The Starling Chronicles

Book One

The Starlings of Ramblewood

By Dash Hoffman

Illustrated by Mark Flower

The Starling Chronicles

Book I

The Starlings of Ramblewood

Written by Dash Hoffman

Illustrated by Mark Flower

Published by Paris Publishing

Copyright 2017 Dash Hoffman

This book is licensed for your personal enjoyment only. This book may not be re-sold or given away to other people. If you would like to share this book with another person, please purchase an additional copy for each recipient. If you're reading this book and did not purchase it, or it was not purchased for your use only, then please return to your favorite book retailer and purchase your own copy. Thank you for respecting the hard work of this author.

Dedications

With enormous gratitude to the members of the
Brown Paper Packages Book Club

Melissa Carleo
Amy Lohrenz
Coni Sanders
Christina Colombo
Melinda Luckay
Tracy Kessner
Leslie Ann Herd
Katie Huber
Kristina Boyce
Kristina Boyce
Charlotte Herring
Mary Zimmerman
Alyssa Rose
Melanie Bryant
Azurayé Mason
Alexandra Herd
Misty Ewegen
Aarthi Arunachalam
Robin Rose

With love and gratitude to Risa Buck, who has made
much of Dash Hoffman's writing possible.

To my mates, Bradley Gibbons, Katy Ordway, and
Jackie Clark, with all my love.

To Kim and Steve Dodd, and Robyn McNicol,
for sharing your own beautiful worlds with me;
I will cherish them always.

Table of Contents

Chapter One - Endings and Beginnings	1
Chapter Two - Mysteries	18
Chapter Three - New York	32
Chapter Four - The Time Palace	51
Chapter Five - The Gypsy Windlass	75
Chapter Six - New Horizons	95
Chapter Seven - Voyagers	120
Chapter Eight - Secrets	133
Chapter Nine - The Port of Morrow	146
Chapter Ten - One	177
Chapter Ten - Two	199
Chapter Ten - Three	208

For Aarthi,
Set your sails for the stars and go on a fantastic adventure!
-Dash Hoffman

Chapter One

~

Endings and Beginnings

The rhythmic swish of a heavy old brass pendulum swayed in sync with the soft tick – tick – ticking of the timeworn grandfather clock that stood sentry near the front door of the apartment. The sounds filled the silent air, thick with grief and confusion.

The apartment was well designed; beautiful furnishings, lofty view of the bustling streets far below, several large windows that let in sunlight, and city light, and a pretty picture of the world outside, save for that moment. At that moment the skies were filled with dark, heavy clouds that were pouring themselves out onto the earth and everything on it.

There was only one person in the apartment; a young girl of fourteen years old. Her green eyes were puffy and rimmed with red, and her lips were slightly swollen from weeping, though she had cried herself out and there were no more tears to be had.

A deep grinding noise emerged from the depths of the grandfather clock as the gears whirred and spun, and golden chimes began to ring out, tolling the hour one beat at a time, like a heartbeat, going, going, gone. It was ten in the morning.

She looked over at the aged piece and her eyes stopped on a carefully trimmed square of paper, yellowed at the edges which curled slightly. She knew the words that were written there; she'd read them countless times, but she read them again, just to see the handwriting of the woman who had composed the letters into words, into a thought shared.

'The irony of time is that it does not exist'

The girl wished with everything in her heart that time did not exist, for if it didn't, things wouldn't change, and everything would stay the same, and her mother would still be there with her.

A strong knock sounded at the door beside the clock. The girl's heart skipped a beat and her eyes flew to the entrance of her home as the handle turned. Her breath quickened as the door opened, but then a flood of relief washed through her when she saw the woman who walked into the room.

The girl was reminded sharply and suddenly of how similar her mother and her Aunt looked. Her mother Marleigh had long, dark brown hair with gentle waves in it, green eyes, olive skin, and a sweet and warm smile. Her Aunt Vianne was not quite as slender as Marleigh, though she was fit. She stood a few inches shorter than her mother, with the same brown hair in big curls that almost reached her shoulders. Her eyes were green as well, her skin olive toned, and her smile which was usually as warm as Marleigh's, was gone that day.

"Jules!" The woman exclaimed as she blinked back tears and pressed her lips together tightly for a moment, "Goodness, it's been so long since I've seen you. You've grown so much. Come hear darling, come here." She held her arms out and for the first time since the news had come about her mother's death, Jules felt some lightness in her grief. The sharing of it with someone who loved her mother as much as she did made the pain more bearable somehow.

Jules sprung from the sofa and into her Aunt's arms, burying her face in the woman's neck and letting her sorrow flow once more. Somehow there were a few more tears that found their way to her cheeks and chin, before leaving her. They held one another tightly for a long minute, and then Vianne let her go and looked down at her.

"Jules, I know this is terrible timing, but there's something that you should know. There's someone that you have to meet right now." Vianne looked as serious as Jules had ever seen her, though she hadn't seen her very often in her growing up years.

Confusion furrowed Jules' brow. "Someone I need to... meet?" She asked quizzically. She couldn't for the life of her imagine who it might be, not so soon after her mother's death.

Vianne stepped aside and Jules drew in a sharp breath of wonder. There, standing behind where Jules had been, was a young boy. He was two inches shorter than Jules, with dark brown hair that lay in modest, gentle curls around his head. He had olive toned skin and his frame was thin but sturdy. Jules stared at his eyes. They were exactly like hers.

"Jules, this is Henry. Henry..." Vianne took a deep breath and let it out slowly, pacing herself. "This is your sister, Jules." Vianne said nothing more then, and the boy and the girl stood silent as well, staring at one another as the clock ticked ever onward.

"Sister?" He whispered, tearing his eyes from Jules and looking up suddenly at Vianne. "I... that can't be. You never told me I had a sister!" The confusion on his face matched that of Jules'.

She frowned and glared at her Aunt. "Is this some kind of joke? I don't have a brother! How could you try to play some kind of joke like this on me, especially today?" Pain stabbed at her heart again and she planted her hands on her hips.

Vianne shook her head slowly and looked from Henry to Jules. "I'm so very sorry. This is no joke. It's as true as can be. You two are brother and sister. I realize this is a shock to you both, but it's true. Marleigh was a mother to both of you, but for your own safety, we separated you two when Henry was born, and you were raised apart from one another. Now… with Marleigh gone, it seems that we have no choice but to put you two together and hope for the best. I'm sure you both have a million questions, but we don't have much time. I'm going to make a pot of tea, and we can talk for a few minutes, but then we have to leave."

With that, Vianne walked into the kitchen, her long, thin, multicolored silk jacket billowing out slightly behind her, almost like a half full sail. Her sweet floral perfume left a scented trail behind her. The clock ticked on in the silence, and Henry and Jules turned to look at each other fully.

They were both still for a long moment, but then she took the first few steps toward him, and in response, he began to walk slowly and carefully toward her, one foot in front of the other.

They stopped just before each other, staring into one another's faces and eyes. Jules and Henry had the same green eyes, just like Vianne's and Marleigh's. Her hair was long and straight, reaching to the middle of her back when it was loose, where his was close cropped to his head, save for the wavy curls at his crown. They looked like slightly different mirror images of each other.

She lifted her hand and held it out to him. "I'm Jules… Jules Starling." She said in a soft voice, trying to wrap her mind around what she was seeing.

He took her hand and gave it a friendly shake. "I'm Henry Starling." He answered quietly. They let go of each other and he raised his hand to his chin and scratched it thoughtfully.

"This is so… bizarre." He said in a soft voice, staring at her. "I never knew you existed. I didn't even know that my mother was alive."

Jules blinked. "What do you mean? Where have you been all this time?"

"I live with Aunt Vianne. I've always lived with her. She told me that my mother was gone, so I was living with her. She's raising me." He blinked and pushed his hands down into the pockets of his khaki pants. He was wearing a navy blue button up shirt that was carefully pressed and tucked into his belted pants, and on his feet he wore dark leather loafers.

It was a smart contrast to Jules' jeans, ankle boots, long sleeved t-shirt, and vest. Her hair was pulled up into a ponytail, and she wore a thin leather strand braided bracelet that she had made herself.

"My mother…" Jules paused a moment, trying to make herself say the strange words, "I mean, *our* mother, just passed away." She shook her head. "This can't be real. This can't be true! You can't be her son. She never would have let you live somewhere else! She would have had you living with us if you were…" She trailed off again, still staring at him, still trying to make any kind of sense of it.

"It's true!" Vianne's voice called from the kitchen.

Henry and Jules both looked over at the doorway to the kitchen and then back at each other. She lifted her chin slightly. "How old are you?"

"I'm twelve." He answered simply. "How old are you?"

She did the math in her head as she replied. "I'm fourteen." She paused a moment. "I don't remember mom being pregnant, but I guess I wouldn't have noticed if I was a year old and change." She sighed in resignation. There was silence between them again as they regarded each other for another long moment.

He frowned slightly. "I'm so sorry to hear that she's gone; that you've lost her. It must be dreadful for you. I… I'm not quite sure how I should feel, I mean, I've lived my whole life thinking that she was gone. I never knew her, but you've always had her, and I can't imagine losing someone you've always had. I'm sorry." He said again.

Jules swallowed the lump that formed in her throat and nodded. "Me too." she whispered. Then she tilted her head a little to the side. Her pony tail shifted slightly. "Do you think this is real? Do you think you're really my brother?"

Henry nodded. "I do. Look at us. It's… it's like looking in the mirror, almost. I don't know how it's possible, but I do believe it."

She shook her head, and her ponytail swung a little. "Then I'm glad." She bit at her lower lip for a moment and drew in a long slow breath to steady herself. When she spoke again, her voice cracked.

"I thought I was going to be alone in the world, except for Aunt Vianne, but I guess I'm not. I guess you're not. I guess… I guess we have each other." She gave him a hopeful look.

He returned a firm nod to her. "We do indeed." He agreed with her.

Before he could add anything else, Vianne called them to the small dining room just off of the kitchen and living room. The strange and tender moment between the newly met siblings broke, and they walked together into the other room.

Tea was waiting on the table; three pretty china cups, sitting neatly in china saucers, set at three places on the dining room table. They each had a cloth napkin and a cookie. Amber colored liquid in the teacups sent off undulating swirls of steam, and the crisp scent of the tea touched delicately at their noses.

Jules and Henry glanced at each other and then looked to Vianne, who was standing behind her chair waiting for them. She gave them each a kind half-smile that didn't quite reach her eyes, and they sat.

She poured milk into her tea and stirred it with a little teaspoon. "I wish you two were meeting under better circumstances, I really do. There's just no way around it now." She said in a quiet voice.

"Why haven't we met before?" Henry asked, giving her a narrow look. "I've spent my whole life with you, thinking my mother was dead already, and never knowing I had a sister in this world. I would have preferred to grow up with them both, not that I'm ungrateful to you for raising me, but they are my family. Or…" He paused with a disappointed look, "they were."

Vianne sighed and Jules felt a surge of relief that Henry had pressed again for more information about them and their strange beginnings. She felt just as he did, that they should always have been together from the beginning.

"You've been kept apart so that you would be safe. Marleigh and I didn't want to do it, but there was no choice in the matter, really. It was the best way to protect you." She sounded tired. Vianne lifted her teacup and took a long sip of her brew.

"How could keeping us apart keep us safe?" Jules questioned suspiciously. "That doesn't make any sense. Who would we need to be kept safe from anyway?" She had never in her life felt as if she was in any danger.

Vianne set her cup back in the saucer and touched both of her forefingers to the rim of it as she spoke, without raising her eyes to look at either of the children.

"You needed to be kept safe from the same people who killed you mother. We thought that separating you and raising you apart would give you a better chance. We were right, I think, but now that my sister is gone, you both need to stay with me, as close to me as possible. It's the only way." She was quiet then as both Henry and Jules stared at her.

Jules tried to find her voice, and after several long moments, she was able to speak just above a whisper. "Killed? She was killed?"

Vianne looked over at her with a pained expression. "They didn't tell you that?" she asked in a soft voice as she reached her hand out to her niece. "I'm so sorry. I thought you knew that. Who told you?"

Jules swallowed hard. "There was an officer at the door this morning. It didn't look like a regular police officer, but he said he was a special investigator. He just said that she…" she nearly choked saying the words as tears stung at her eyes again, "that she died at work. He said someone would come for me, but he didn't say who. He told me to wait here, so I did. Then you came."

It had been the worst morning of her whole life, and the only thing that had improved it was the arrival of her Aunt, and the boy who was sitting across from her watching her with sorrowful eyes.

Vianne shook her head slowly. "I'm so sorry honey. I thought they told you."

"They?" Jules frowned slightly.

"I mean he." Vianne looked away and waved her hand dismissively. "Well, we need to look to the immediate future for now. You'll be coming to live with Henry and me right away. I have a room ready for you. You'll just need to pack your things, and we'll go."

Jules looked down at her tea, staring at it. It had cooled enough that there was no more steam coming off of it. She was going to have to pack and leave her home, just as fast as that, and there was nothing to be done about it.

"I have so many questions." Henry filled the silence with his curiosity, looking from his sister to Vianne.

Vianne gave him a half-hearted smile. "Not today, dear. We will have lots of time to talk it all through. Today we need to focus on the necessary changes and nothing else."

Henry looked back over at Jules. "Would you like some help packing?" he offered kindly.

She raised her eyes to meet his. She didn't know what to say at first, but then she realized that she wanted to have the last few moments of her life in her home where she and her mother had lived together, just to herself.

"I appreciate you offering, but I think I'll just go pack my own things." She tried to sound polite, and she hoped that he would understand.

Henry gave her a nod and a sympathetic look, and she knew then that she was going to like having him in her life. He did get it. He got her, and that was an enormous and helpful relief.

She didn't feel like eating or drinking anything, but she made herself swallow the tea that was sitting before her, and then she excused herself from the table and pushed her chair in.

Giving her Aunt a curious look, she said quietly, "What's going to happen to everything here that isn't mine? What about my mom's stuff?"

Vianne sighed and shook her head. "Someone else will come to get it, and we'll go through it later on. We don't need to make all of the changes at once. We'll do it a step at a time, and that will make it easier." She reached her hand out to Jules' and pressed her fingers warmly against Jules' hand.

"I know things are at their darkest now, but that only means that the road ahead has light that will heal you over time. It will heal all of us. You'll survive, and beautiful times will come again. For now, do little things, and the big things will be taken care of as we go along."

Jules nodded and walked through the living room and down the hallway to her bedroom. She stood in the doorway, looking around at her personal space in her home. There was a dresser with a few feminine figurines on it. There were pictures and posters on the walls of places around the world that she had either gone to with her mother or wanted to go to someday. Most of them were sites yet unseen by her. Dreams of lands to discover.

There were shelves with books; lots of books. Her mother had insisted on homeschooling her, and they had studied almost everything under the sun, it seemed like. She considered taking all of them, but she'd read them each several times, and she guessed that they would wind up at her Aunt's house eventually anyway.

She had a few stuffed animals on her bed, and she thought about taking them, but something in her heart told her that her childhood days were done in the biggest way, and that her life would never ever be the same again.

As she looked at the trinkets and toys that were set about here and there in her tidied room, she slowly became aware that most of what she was looking at wasn't anything that she was going to want to keep or take with her. It was all just stuff. None of it would bring her mother back. All of it brought memories to her, but the memories were there whether or not she had the stuff.

The weight of the pain in her heart and the worry on her mind made her need to go light; it made her want to let go of everything that she didn't absolutely have to have.

Taking her shoulder bag, she pushed a few small things into it that she did want to keep, and she pulled a small suitcase out of the closet and filled it with the clothes she would need and a book she had been reading, 'Journey to the Center of the Earth'. It was written by a man who had the same name as her, 'Jules Verne'. She liked that fact as much as she liked the story.

With a long last look around, Jules held in the sob that wanted to sound from her throat and she forced her aching heart to keep beating. She took a deep breath and whispered, "Goodbye, old life." Turning away from it, she went out to the living room to see her Aunt and her brother waiting for her.

It was the strangest sensation she had ever known, walking out of her home for what would be the last time, locking the door behind her and knowing that the key on the little braided keychain that she had made would never slip into the lock and open the home up again.

She left with her family and did not turn around to look back over her shoulder. She was leaving and it was done. All she had was the road ahead of her, and she wanted nothing more at that moment than to keep her eyes on it.

***

They boarded a train and Henry and Jules sat across from one another beside the window. They watched silently out of the glass as the train passed through the chaotic noise of the city and through the seemingly unending rows of houses set on alternating streets, one after the other.

Finally the boxy houses gave way to patches of trees and wide open land in the countryside, and to long slim fences that rose and fell on the hills that flew past the train.

The day was wet everywhere, from the city to the suburbs, and raindrops that hit the train trailed into long thin lines, seeming to streak into the past right behind Jules, where her own tears appeared to have gone, leaving nothing in her to weep further.

As the train began to pull into the countryside, the dark clouds thinned and then broke apart, and golden shafts of sunlight filtered through them, overtaking them. By the time they were deep into the country, there was no more rain; nothing but a beautiful warm day.

Vianne stood up as the train came to one of its many stops, and the children followed her out of the car and onto the platform. The train station before them was nothing like the loud, dirty, noisy stations in the city. This one was small and made of wood, with a charming old style to it, as if it was from another century and hadn't noticed that the rest of the world had gone racing by into a much more modern future.

Despite her bleak mood, Jules noticed the modest place and liked it. It seemed cheery and welcoming, and that was a balm to her raw soul.

'*Sea Mist Cove*' read the tidy sign that hung from the sheltering roof over the platform. Jules blinked as she read it and she realized for the first time that while she had seen her Aunt Vianne a handful of times over the years as she had grown, she had never been to her home, and she had no idea where her Aunt lived. She had only known that her Aunt and her mother would meet up now and then for brief visits.

"Is that the name of the town here? Is this where you live?" Jules asked, turning her eyes from the trim little sign to her Aunt.

Vianne nodded and gave her a smile. "It is. It's a spot of a town, but it has everything we need, and it's quite a lovely place to live. Henry enjoys it, don't you Henry?"

He shrugged lightly. "I wish it had a bigger library, but I do enjoy it. We live near the beach on the far side of the cove, so we don't really have any close neighbors. It's really private, which I like, and quiet. I do love walking along the beach at low tide. It's like treasure hunting."

Vianne ruffled her fingers over the brown curls atop his head and laughed softly. "I don't think there's a library big enough for you on this earth."

Henry chuckled quietly. "I think you're right." He turned to Jules then and held his hand out to take her suitcase. "Can I carry that for you?"

She only held back for a moment before handing it to him. "Thanks." She said, adjusting the shoulder bag she had slung at an angle over her torso. She wasn't used to having help, but as she watched her brother picking up the suitcase, she realized it might be nice to have someone to share her time, troubles, and joys with.

He gave her an encouraging look. "I think you'll really like it here. It's nice. At least, I hope you'll like it here."

Vianne took them to her car, parked near the train station, and then drove them down the road and past the edge of the town.

Sea Mist Cove gave the impression that someone with a fanciful imagination had painted it on a warm summer day in a pleasant mood, and then breathed onto the painting and brought it all to life. There were small shops lining the main street, streetlamps that were elegantly and intricately designed as if from another era, flowers in pretty pots and hanging baskets set all about, and from where Jules could see, the whole town looked as if it was clean from top to bottom. There was no gum on the sidewalks or trash on the street. There were no long lines of cars honking at each other or billows of smoke coming from any buildings. It was a sweet town, and it made Jules feel calm and peaceful, which she hadn't expected at all.

Vianne drove them past the community and up and down a few hills until the narrow road turned right, and she turned left, pulling onto a winding lane that led over more green hills and past trees filled with leaves that seemed to dance in the ocean breeze.

Jules squinted a little as she looked out of the car window, letting that same breeze wash over her face and tug teasingly at the end of her ponytail. She could taste the sea salt on her lips and she watched the way the afternoon light danced lambent across the tops of the waves, glittering as if the whole sea were diamonds.

When they came to a crest in the hill, she could easily see why the town had been named as it had. There was a big cove, almost a full circle, ringed with hills that were covered in trees, where the sea came in gently and washed up on a golden sandy shore, and that's where the town was built.

Beyond the cove, right outside of it, the sea seemed to take over the rest of the world, stretching out to the horizon so far that the blue of the water and the blue of the sky seemed to become one.

"Here we are." Vianne said with a tired smile as she came around the last curve and the trees along the road opened up fully into a wide clearing.

An arched sign made of filigree metalwork and looking as if it had been created in the 1800's, stood guard over the road. There was a word on it, and Jules ducked her head down to look through the windshield of the car to read it just before they passed beneath it.

'Ramblewood'

"What's Ramblewood?" Jules asked, as the home and grounds came into clear view.

"This whole place is Ramblewood. The house, the grounds, the small forest we just drove through, the beach just down the hill there behind the house… this is all Ramblewood. It's an estate, actually, but that sounds so pretentious to me, that we skip that and keep it simple. Ramblewood is home, and that's where we live." Vianne made it sound so matter-of-fact that Jules could almost sense the hominess of it.

As she got out of the car and stood before the home, she drew in a deep breath and gazed in wonder. All of it entranced her from the first view. The house was two and a half stories tall, the architecture all Victorian and absolutely pristine.

On the first level there was a wide wraparound porch that ran the length of the house, with arched latticework and a delicately carved railing. There were big windows all the way around it, hung with lace curtains. The front door was at the corner of the house, and that whole corner had a regal and welcoming style to it.

On the second level there was another deck, with a short metal railing, that spanned the length and width of the deck below it. A rounded room came off of one side of the house, with five windows on the second level, and a grandly carved turret at the top of it, almost as if someone had placed a large dollop of chocolate cream atop the house. Above the front corner of the house there arose a tower, almost in the style of a French chateau, with smaller windows that looked out on all sides, and it was crowned with a small squared deck.

The grounds all around the house were immaculately kept; the green grass and hedges and trees trimmed, the flowers and bushes set about just so and tenderly cared for. It was the finest, prettiest, most exotic and mysterious house that Jules had ever seen. She was astounded at the sight of it.

"This is where you live?" She asked, not taking her eyes from it.

"This is where we live." Vianne replied with a kind smile, wrapping her arm around Jules' shoulders. "I know this is the worst day of your life, but tomorrow will be the first day of your new life, and this will be a good home to have a new life in. You will find some happiness here. You will have a family here, and you will be at home here as long as you like. Welcome, my darling. Welcome to Ramblewood."

Ramblewood

Chapter Two

~

Mysteries

Vianne and Henry brought Jules into the house and they stopped in the wide, octagonal foyer. There were two wide doorways that led off from it; one to the left and the other to the right, and directly across from the big oak front door, there was a broad staircase with a white wooden railing that wound up from the floor in a gradual curve to the upper level.

The floors and steps were all hardwood in lighter tones, glossed to a sheen, though there were colorful Arabian and Oriental rugs over much of the areas. A great crystal chandelier hung in the voluminous space over the foyer.

"I think we'll have a light dinner in the kitchen nook, and then we'll call it a night. It's been a long, dreadful day, and we all need some rest. Henry, you can show Jules around the house tomorrow while I'm at work." Vianne took a few steps toward the staircase. "Let's get you settled into your room, shall we?"

Henry and Jules followed Vianne up the steps, rounding them to the second floor. There was a landing that spread out to a long hallway that was split into a V-shape.

"I thought I'd put you in the turret room." Vianne said, heading down the hall. "There's a nice view of the ocean and the beach from there, and Henry's room is just down the hall in the tower over the foyer, so he's close."

Jules was surprised, and she felt the slightest glimmer of curiosity and what might be the corner of the edge of happiness at being put in such an elegant place.

The room was expansive in the width and height of it, as the turret was open spaced as well, with a twisting spiral light that hung from the center of it. The windows were tall with arches at the top of them and lace curtains over the glass. The bed stood at a wall that was beside a solitary window, and it was covered in a thick, white, cotton duvet, and stacked with deep pillows of varying sizes. A wooden desk was set against the far wall, topped with a stained glass Tiffany lamp and a brand new computer. The computer seemed like an anomaly in such a classically designed home.

Vianne opened a door on the wall and headed into the walk-in closet, turning on the light inside. "This is all yours. I know you didn't bring much, but I think we'll wind up filling up some of this space with your things, and you can make it your own over time. There's no rush. Just be comfortable now." She left the closet and opened another door that led to a private bathroom with a claw-foot tub and a standalone shower. White tile lined the floor and matched a white counter and cabinetry in the room, making everything look brighter.

Jules could scarcely take it all in. She stood in the room, looking all around it in awe, and then walked over to the cushy armchair beside one of the windows and sank down into it.

"It is the worst day of my life." She said in a soft tone, looking at Vianne as Henry set the suitcase down on the wooden chest at the end of the bed. "This takes some of the edge off. Thank you for… for everything." She managed to finish as she felt emotion rising in her again.

Vianne went to her and hugged her warmly, holding her for a long moment before she let her go and looked down at her. "Henry and I are going to make dinner. Come down to the kitchen whenever you're ready. It's just to the left when you come off of the stairs."

They left her alone, though as Henry walked out, he gave her a lasting glance over his shoulder, and she could see that he looked worried about her.

Jules unpacked her suitcase and stored the case in the closet. She wandered around her new room, feeling as if she was in a dream. Going to the window, she opened it and a rush of cool ocean breeze danced in the curtains and swept over her, calming her. She closed her eyes as she took it into her lungs.

It had been the strangest day of her life. She had lost her mother and found a brother she never knew she had. Then she had moved to a new home, all in a matter of hours. She left the window open and went back down the hall and the stairs to the foyer. Her Aunt and brother had dinner ready, and it was simple and just right for her. They ate a hot soup with soft bread and tea. Jules didn't feel hungry, but the soup smelled and tasted good, and when the meal was over, exhaustion overtook her, and she said goodnight to her family and went to bed.

Her sleep was so deep that there were no dreams, or at least, none that she could remember when she awoke in the morning. Before she opened her eyes, she could hear the distant crashing of the waves on the sand, and she opened her eyes and looked around the room. It was even prettier than it had been the day before. The sunlight was warm and bright, the day was new, and though her mother was gone, she somehow didn't feel alone.

A fast shower and dressing, and she stepped out into the hall. She saw Henry's door open at the end of the hallway, and she walked quietly to it, hoping he was there and awake.

She peered in, and saw him sitting in an armchair as cushy as hers was, near the window in his room, with a book in his hands and his nose buried in the pages.

"Henry?" she asked hesitantly.

The boy looked up at her presently, and closed the book as a cautious smile overtook his face. "How are you feeling?" He asked, setting the book down on the small table beside him.

"I'm… in a weird place." She answered honestly.

"So am I." He replied. "I made breakfast if you're hungry. I waited for you, so we could eat together if you want to." The corner of his mouth turned up a little and there was a light in his green eyes. He pushed his hands down into his pockets as he watched her hopefully.

Jules felt an unexpected warmth in her heart that began to grow just a bit. She nodded. "Okay. That sounds good. Thank you."

Looking as if he was trying not to be too anxious, Henry walked swiftly across the room, one foot in front of the other, and led her down the stairs and into the kitchen again, going to the nook where they had eaten dinner.

"Normally we eat dinner in the dining room, just beyond those doors," he told her, pointing to a set of pocket doors at the end of the room, "but Aunt Vianne wanted to keep it simple. We usually have breakfast in here." He set out a cheese plate with four kinds of cheeses, grapes, strawberries, honey, and two kinds of breads, as well as a ceramic pot of oatmeal and two dishes of yogurt. "I didn't know what you like, so I kind of raided the fridge for a bit of everything."

He looked uncertain and Jules gave him a half smile. "This looks great, thank you." She sat down with him and he breathed out a sigh of relief.

"Where is Aunt Vianne, anyway?" Jules asked as she took the teapot from Henry.

"She went to work." He stated flatly as he buttered some bread.

"Where does she work?" Jules asked, pouring milk into her tea.

He frowned. "That's an interesting question, actually. She works in the garden most every day, but I never see her out there."

Jules blinked in confusion. "Doesn't she have a job?"

Henry looked slightly confused. "I… I guess so. She has an office here, on one side of the library. I'll show you that when I give you the tour, but she's not usually in it. She doesn't leave to go to work, except to work in the greenhouse and the garden."

"But you never see her in the garden…" Jules finished for him.

"Right." He answered, chewing thoughtfully on his bite of bread. He swallowed and looked over at his sister. "What did… mom… do?" He asked, finding it strange to say the word 'mom'.

Jules felt as if a weight was crushing her heart. She sighed and her shoulders slumped. "She… well, she had an office at the apartment, and she worked out of the office. I'm not really sure what she did. She didn't talk with me about it, she just went to work in there sometimes, and I wasn't allowed in, and when she was done working, she'd come out."

Henry frowned thoughtfully. "So neither of them really work at say, an office or a business outside of home, really."

She shook her head. "I guess not. She was nearly always there. She homeschooled me, so I didn't meet a lot of other kids, though we had outings all the time."

Henry looked as if he was suddenly piqued with enormous interest. "I'm homeschooled too! Aunt Vianne teaches me. It's astounding how much she knows. I don't feel that I'm missing anything I'd be getting at a public school, aside from a group of friends, I guess. I am in some reading groups at the library in town, and I am on a rowing team, so I have a few friends, but we stay pretty close to home. Where did you go on outings?"

"Museums and art galleries, historical places, old battlegrounds and state capitals, things like that." She answered, reaching for some cheese and grapes.

"It's fascinating." He shook his head and picked up his teacup, staring at it as his mind became a whir with the information they were sharing.

"What's fascinating?" She asked, nibbling on some cheese.

He set his teacup down and looked squarely at her. "Don't you see? We were kept apart from each other right from the beginning, but we were raised the same way by sisters. We're both homeschooled, they both work at home, and we are both kept close to them and apart from each other. That's just so… interesting to me. I feel like we've been kept behind a wall. Carefully kept, if that makes any sense. I mean, look at what Aunt Vianne said yesterday; they wanted to keep us apart because they had to, until now when there is no choice, and she said she wants to keep us both as close to her as possible. Like she's guarding us from something. Like they've both been guarding us. See what I mean?"

Jules frowned, too. "I do see what you mean. That is strange." She furrowed her brow and thought on it for a long minute. "Why do you think they'd do that?"

He shook his head slowly. "Honestly, I have no idea."

"You live here, is there anything strange or unusual about this place?" She asked, eyeing him curiously as she sipped her tea.

"You mean other than the place itself? Although, it doesn't seem too strange to me; it's home, but I'm well aware that no one else we know lives like we do." He shook his head and shrugged. "I don't think I've seen anything here that's too out of place."

"Other than Aunt Vianne working in the garden and you never seeing her there? That's weird." Jules couldn't make it out at all. If she worked there, of course she could be seen working there.

Henry was quiet a moment as he considered it. "I guess not. We study, we go to town, we have meals together, she goes to work in the garden or the greenhouse. Sometimes she comes out looking a bit worse for the wear, and she tells me she's had a hard day of it in the garden, but that's it."

Jules was quiet then for a long moment. "Do you think your life will change much with me being here?" She asked, wondering what kind of impact her presence was really going to have.

He smiled at her. "I hope it does. I'm glad you're here, and I want to tell you, I thought about us all night and all morning. Even though we didn't grow up together, I want you to know that I will always be there for you, no matter what."

Jules felt as if her heart had healed in more ways than she ever knew it could. She swallowed the tears that sprang to her eyes. "I'll always be there for you no matter what too. I promise."

They shared a smile and he handed her a fig drizzled with honey. "So what was mom like? Do you mind me asking?"

Jules didn't know what to say at first. She didn't know how to describe a person succinctly. "Mom was strong and smart. She was a really determined lady; it seemed like everything she set her mind to, she did, even if it took a little while. She wouldn't give up on things. She was kind and she tried to be funny a lot, though I didn't think she was very funny, but maybe that was me. She used to read books to me all the time. She'd lay in my bed with me and read stories I hadn't heard yet, or sometimes get back into old favorites, but usually we read new ones. I loved that."

He stared at her, imagining himself in her place, wondering what it would be like for his mother to read a story to him. "It sounds pretty incredible." He said quietly.

"What is it like growing up with Aunt Vianne?" Jules returned the question to him.

"It's fun, but she keeps a close eye on me. I don't really mind it; I have no interest in getting into trouble, but it always feels like there's an invisible fence around this home and around me, keeping me back from… from I don't know what." He sighed and gave his head a little shake.

"So mysterious." Jules gave him a little smile. "Maybe we should just go out to the garden and the greenhouse and see what she's up to. Maybe she could use some help out there." She couldn't see why Henry hadn't thought of that.

He shook his head adamantly. "Oh no, we can't. I'm not allowed out there. The greenhouse is strictly off limits."

She pushed her lower lip out as she considered what he said. "Kind of like mom keeping me out of her office in the apartment. So strange."

They continued to talk as they finished their breakfast, and she helped him do the dishes and put them all away.

With breakfast out of the way, he took her on a tour of the house. First through the dining room which was a sophisticated looking space with dark wood paneled walls and crystal chandeliers, along with a long dark wooden dining table and matching chairs all around it.

Next he showed her the library, which was good sized, with a thick, soft sofa and a big fireplace. "We always have fires going in here in the wintertime, and I spend a lot of time in here. Sometimes she lets me have tea in here, if I'm in the middle of an important study assignment or a really great book." He gave her a smile and then took her through the library to Vianne's office.

There was a computer on the desk and a printer nearby. There were photos of Marleigh and Vianne as younger women in a frame on the desk. Jules looked around the room and planted her hands on her hips, casing the place with an eagle eye.

Henry paused and watched her. "Do you see anything unusual?"

She twisted her mouth and shook her head. "No, this place is exceptionally ordinary." She frowned a little. "This is an old house, are there any secret doors or anything?"

Henry nodded. "Yes, but nothing connected to this room, and nothing too exciting. They just go to other rooms in the house."

He took her through to the music room, which was the downstairs half of the turret room. There was a baby grande piano near the rounded windows, and there were other instruments set in stands or on shelves throughout the room. A viola, a violin, a saxophone, a harp, a clarinet, a French horn, various drums from around the world, and an ancient looking harpsichord.

Jules gazed about, impressed. "Does she play all of these?"

Henry ran his fingers over the keys on the piano. "We both do. She's taught me to play all of them. We play together nearly every day."

She smiled again and looked at him with tremendous respect. "That's amazing. I only know the piano a bit."

He smiled back. "You'll learn the rest. You're here now with us. We'll teach you." He brightened then and looked at her hopefully. "Would you like to play a piece with me?"

She nodded and they sat down together on the bench at the piano. After a few tries, they had it figured out, and they played a bit of Beethoven together, discovering that they had a shared passion for music, and much more in common than they realized. Jules hadn't expected to find herself feeling happy ever again, but sitting there with her brother at the piano, playing along with him at his side, she realized that she did feel some happiness, and she was grateful for it.

After a while they left the music room and he took her through the drawing room and back up the stairs. There were other rooms to see there, though most of them were bedrooms. Jules learned that her Aunt had collected various treasures from all over the world, from many different countries and times, and they were beautifully displayed throughout her home.

The siblings went for a long walk down away from the house and along the beach, talking about everything and getting to know one another. They found that they had so much in common, much more than they would have guessed, and they found that they each had a good friend in the other, for which they were both profoundly glad.

Jules picked up seashells along the way as they walked, and when they got back to the house, Henry took her to his room and gave her a delicately carved wooden box to put them all in. She took it to her room and set it on one of the small tables near the window. Looking at it, she remembered Vianne telling her just the day before that she would make the room her own and fill it with her own things soon enough, and she rested her hand on the box of sea shells and felt a little pleased. She would make this place her home, a little at a time, and she would be happy there, someday.

Henry and Jules spent the day together, and decided to surprise Vianne with a dinner ready-made for her. They prepared the meal and waited, and the hours ticked by, but there was no sign of her in the gardens, and no sign of anyone in the greenhouse, not that they could see through the panes of it very well, especially from the house.

The dinner hour had passed, and though they were talking and enjoying each other's company, both of them were becoming worried that Vianne had been gone too long. She hadn't even come in for lunch.

Finally, Jules paused in their conversation to say something about it. "She's been gone an awfully long time. I mean, I haven't even seen her today. She should have been in at some point, shouldn't she?"

"I think so, yes. She's not usually gone this long." Henry answered, biting at his lower lip.

"Well, we have dinner ready and I'm beginning to get worried. I know you said we aren't supposed to go out to the greenhouse, but she gave you that rule. She never said a word about it to me, at least not yet, so

I'm going to go out there and see if I can find her. I want to at least make sure she's okay." She stood up and headed for the door.

"You shouldn't go! We should wait here for her." He pleaded as he stood up.

"Henry, it's really late and she's been gone all day. I don't mind if she isn't pleased with me for going out there; I just want to make sure she's okay." Jules gave him a solemn look. "You can stay here if you want to, then you won't get in trouble and it will just be me, and I'll even tell her that I didn't know I shouldn't go out there."

He shook his head and pushed his hands down into his pants pockets. "No, that's alright. I'll go with you. I'm worried too. It has been too long."

Together they walked outside and down a pretty path through the gorgeous gardens at the side of the house. There were flowers and trees and bushes of every kind, and even a little pond. Just as they were coming to the greenhouse, which was down a little hill from the main house, Jules saw Henry reach his hand out and touch a beautiful old lamppost by the path.

"That's pretty." She said, looking up at it as it glowed in the golden late afternoon light.

"It always makes me think of Narnia." Henry told her with a grin. "I do love that series."

She smiled and nodded. "Me too." She replied as they reached the door of the greenhouse. They both stopped and hesitated, looking at each other.

"Are you sure you want to go in? I can go in alone and look for her. She probably won't be as mad at me, but you know the rules. Maybe you should wait out here?" She suggested helpfully.

Henry shook his head resolutely. "No, I'm going in with you."

Taking a deep breath she nodded. "Okay then. Let's go."

Reaching for the door handle, she turned it and they walked into the greenhouse together. It was a tall white framed structure with squares of glass all over it, most of them refracting the light of the sinking sun into rainbows all over the place. Inside there were tables and shelves lined with plants of many different species and sizes. There were a few work benches in the back.

The children walked slowly through all of the greenery, looking for their Aunt. They went down one aisle between tables and plants, and reached the end of the greenhouse, then turned and headed back down the other aisle going up the opposite side of the way they'd just gone.

"I don't see her, do you?" Jules asked, looking around carefully.

"No, I don't." Henry answered, wondering how he had lived at the house all his life and never gone inside the greenhouse before, regardless of the rules, but then again, he just wasn't a rule breaker.

They reached the other end of the greenhouse and came back to the front of it again. "She's not here." Jules said with a deep frown. "This is so strange."

Henry raised his brows a bit. "Maybe she went back up to the house while we were walking through here. Maybe we didn't hear the door. It is pretty quiet."

Jules nodded. "Okay. We'll head back up to the house and see if she's back up there."

She reached for the door handle and stopped, frozen where she stood, staring at it.

Henry saw her and his heartbeat picked up. "What? What is it? What's wrong?"

Jules shook her head slowly and reached her hand forward to the door handle. There, hanging on it, was a long brassy looking thin chain; a necklace, with a pendant at the end of it. She curled her fingertips around it and lifted it from the door.

"This… this necklace, it was mom's." She spoke reverently, holding it up and looking at it with a pained expression.

"Hold on, Aunt Vianne's got one just like that." He said, blinking at it. He leaned closer and furrowed his brow a bit.

"No, this one was mom's. I know it. She always wore it; she never took it off. What's it doing here?" She asked, her heart pierced with pain anew as she held the precious token in her hands.

Without another word, she slipped the chain over her neck, feeling somehow closer to her mother as she did so, and holding the pendant in her hand.

It was a little round 3D brass globe, with detailed outlines of the countries of the world and the latitudes and longitudes engraved into it. Around the globe, at a small distance, was a thin ring, like one of Saturn's rings, forming the equator horizontally around the sphere, and there was another ring just like the first, running vertically around the globe, just like a prime meridian and only intersecting with the equatorial ring. It was as if the brass globe inside was suspended within the rings.

"This is mom's." Jules repeated, studying it closely. "I saw her wear this every day."

Henry leaned closer to get a better look. "Oh, you know what, Aunt Vianne's is just a little different. Hers is similar, but it has different markings along the two planes around the sphere. Hers is engraved with strange looking marks just here," he reached his finger out and touched the plane, and as he did there was a flash of white light, and everything around them vanished into blackness.

Chapter Three

~

New York

The blackness faded almost as fast as it had engulfed them, and Henry and Jules gasped, standing frozen just as they had been standing in the greenhouse a moment before, though they were not in the greenhouse any longer.

In the space of a breath the greenhouse had vanished, and they discovered they were both standing on wet cobblestone. It was a narrow road, encased between two tall buildings about three stories tall each, that were matched by more buildings just a little further down the road.

They turned their heads slowly as they looked around themselves, trying to take in the scene about them and absorb it all. Henry reached for Jules' hand.

"What... what just happened? Are you seeing this?" Jules whispered as they stared at the windows and doors and shops down along the road. "Or am I dreaming?"

"I'm seeing an old, old city. Is that what you see?" Henry asked in a whisper.

"I see it. Cobblestone road, brick buildings?" She asked him in return.

"Yeah." He answered, swallowing hard, though his throat was dry.

"Where are we?" She asked worriedly.

He spoke in a low tone. "I think the better question is *when* are we?"

Her head spun and Jules blinked at him. "What?"

"Didn't you notice? There aren't any cars here. Those are horse drawn carriages. Look at the way people are dressed. This looks like what I've seen in books and movies from a century ago. I don't think we're in our time anymore." He said quietly.

Jules looked around closer then, and noticed that everything he had said was true. Every female she saw was wearing a long dress and a hat and gloves, and every man was dressed well in fine coats with hats and most had walking canes. There were no cars, there were only horse drawn carriages. There was nothing around them that was from their time.

"Oh... my... g-" Jules started to say, but Henry clamped a hand over her mouth.

"Shh. We need to get out of sight and figure this out." He said in a hushed voice. "We obviously aren't from here. It may be intuition, but I feel like the last thing we want to do is make a scene and attract attention to ourselves."

"You're probably right." She agreed, finally turning back to him with wide eyes and a pale face.

He looked about quickly and spied an alley closer to the end of the street. "Let's get over there. Quietly. Quickly. We'll be out of sight and we can figure out what's going on."

Just as they turned to head to the alley, a man's voice called out, and they froze in their tracks and looked behind them.

"You there! Urchins! What are you up to at this time of night and dressed so... my word! Is that a young lady in trousers?" The man was in coattails and a top hat. He was staring aghast at Jules.

"Too late." Jules grumbled under her breath. "Let's run!"

"See here! Police! After them!" the man shouted, waving his walking stick at them as he began to give chase to them. It seemed only a moment before two policemen were at his heels, chasing right along with him.

Hand in hand they ran, holding fast to one another as their footfalls landed loudly on the stones at their feet. The men chasing them had nearly caught up to them and they were just about at the alley when they heard a voice; the voice of a young girl, calling to them.

"Oy! You two, don't go that way, they'll get you sure! You'd best follow me! This way, now!" She seemed to appear out of a shadow; a thin little girl, much younger than both of them. She had black hair, hanging in two long braids over her shoulders. She looked wiry, but strong, and the expression on her face was intense.

Henry and Jules shared a split second glance, each of them questioning the other as to whether or not they should listen to the young girl.

"'That's a dead end anyway! Let's go!" she insisted, urging them again as a vaguely Irish accent came out.

Jules gave Henry a nod and he agreed. They glanced back over their shoulders for a second and saw the men nearly upon them. Without another moment of hesitation they bolted after the young girl who seemed almost like a ghost, zipping down a different alley, turning here and then there, ducking down and crawling under piles of crates and rushing through darkened and narrow passageways.

She finally stopped at the edge of an alley that opened out onto what looked to be a main street. They were all breathless and panting, but she looked back behind them and heaved a sigh, her small shoulders sagging as she leaned her back against the wall of the building beside them.

"They're gone." She breathed shortly, looking up at them fully for the first time.

Henry and Jules stared at her. "Thank you, thank you so much." Jules gasped, holding her hand to her ribs.

"Where are we?" Henry asked, doubled over slightly. "What city is this?"

The girl frowned at them. "You don't know what city you're in?" She asked in amazement. Henry and Jules shook their heads.

Shaking her head, the girl lifted her chin slightly. "You're in New York."

Jules cleared her throat and tried to look casual as she asked the other question of utmost importance in her mind. "Um... what year is it?" She lifted one of her brows a bit.

The girl gave them a level stare. "'Have you hit your heads? It's 1849."

Henry and Jules looked at each other with wide eyes and gaped. "How did..." he began, but she only shook her head a little.

"Now I've got some questions for you!" The girl asked, her eyes piercing them. "Who are you and where might you be from?"

"I'm Henry, and this is my sister, Jules." Henry answered. "We're from... the countryside north of here. There's a little seaside town there where we live." He cleared his throat. "We just haven't been here in a while." He looked at her pointedly.

"Who might you be, please?" He asked politely.

"I'm Fiona Murphy, but everyone calls me Finn." She answered, looking as if she hadn't quite made her mind up about the two before her. "I saw you..." She paused a moment. "I was there, just down the road a bit, and I saw you. You came out of nowhere. One minute there was nothing, then the next minute there you was, standing there looking like you couldn't be more lost."

Jules sighed and glanced quickly over at Henry, not exactly sure what they should tell Finn. "Well, you're right, we aren't from here. We're really grateful for your help, though. We'd never have made it without your help. They'd have caught us for certain."

Finn agreed and crossed her arms over her chest. "That's the truth." She eyed them curiously then. "Not that I'm one to talk, but you're sure dressed funny. What's a girl like you doing in trousers?" She looked at Jules.

Finn was in a raggedy dress herself, and she had tattered old worn out shoes on that looked as if they were too big for her. She looked scruffy, and a bit rough and tumble, as if she might be more than a little familiar with living on the streets.

Jules bit at her bottom lip a moment. "Well, where we come from, this is how everyone dresses. I mean, girls wear dresses too, sometimes, but I think most of the time they like to wear pants."

Finn's eyes widened. "'You must be from pretty far away."

"You have no idea." Henry sighed heavily. He furrowed his brow. "Is there somewhere safe where my sister and I could go to be alone? We need to talk."

Finn shook her head. "'You won't get far dressed that way. It's best you stay here for now." She looked from one to the other of them. "What is it like where you live?"

Jules was busy thinking about how they had gotten to New York in 1849, and she wasn't paying too much attention to the young girl in front of her. She answered offhandedly. "It's as different as you could possibly imagine."

"Is it better?" Finn asked, peering at them keenly.

Henry's eyes widened a bit. "In many ways, yes. This is an important time and place, as all are, but things are much better in almost every way. Do you have electricity yet?"

Finn frowned and gave him a skeptical look. "What's lectricy?"

Henry's face fell. "I knew it. Electricity won't be around for another thirty years, I think. I was just reading about this era and I'm fairly positive about that."

Finn's eyes narrowed. "Where did you say you're from?"

He sighed. "Very far away. We need to figure out how to get back there."

"Well, I'll be the first to say I don't know everything, but I've never seen anyone travel the way you did." She nodded at them adamantly.

Jules was busy pacing back and forth a few steps, her thumb under her chin and her fingers over her mouth. She was focused with laser beam intensity, but not on anything around her.

"How are you doing Jules?" Henry asked, looking at her in concern.

"I'm thinking." She mumbled pensively. "I'm retracing our steps. We were in the greenhouse. We walked the whole length of it, we didn't touch anything, and we didn't see anything."

"Right. Then we went to the door to leave." Henry added, watching her

Finn put one hand on her hip and looked up at Henry. "How do they treat orphans where you're from?"

Henry blinked and looked over at her distractedly. "Orphans? Well, I guess like anyone else. They aren't mistreated, most of the time."

Her interest was piqued. She kept her big brown eyes on him. "What about Irish folk?" She asked, pressing further.

"What?" He asked, taking his eyes from his sister once more to look at Finn. "Irish?"

"Aye. How are they treated?" Finn asked, in an almost challenging way.

"Just like everyone else I suppose. I haven't seen or heard otherwise." Henry answered her and then turned back to Jules, who was still pacing and going over their steps.

"What were we doing when it happened?" She asked, running her fingers up and down the chain around her neck. She stopped suddenly and looked down at the pendant, staring at it.

Taking the little globe into her hands, she frowned and began to turn it over and over in her fingers, studying it. "We were looking at this. Then you asked me about it-"

"I touched it." He interjected, his eyes searching hers as they spoke.

"Do you think that…" She asked, holding the brass globe up in her hands and feeling her heart begin to pound in her chest.

"That just might be how we got here. It's worth a try, isn't it?" He asked, looking hopefully at her.

"But I don't know how we did it, if that was it." She lowered a brow doubtfully.

"Are you leaving? To go back where you came from?" Finn asked, looking at them both with wide eyes.

They were only looking at each other. Henry took a breath and almost held it. "With any luck." He replied quietly.

Henry took Jules by the hand and their eyes met for a moment as they both reached for the globe, touching it at the same time.

"Take us home to Ramblewood." Jules said loudly, closing her eyes tight and hoping with everything in her that it would work.

"Not without me!" Cried Finn, launching herself at them and planting her hands on each of their arms.

There was a flash of light and everything went dark. A scream surrounded them, and a moment later, they found themselves standing precisely where they had been standing in the greenhouse when they left.

Everything was the same, except for one thing, and that was the young Irish girl clutching both Jules' and Henry's arms, her eyes shut tight, her mouth open, and a scream still sounding from her. The scream died out and she opened her eyes slowly to find the two older children looking at her.

Panic was written across her face as Finn slowly turned her head to look around her. Henry and Jules were gaping open mouthed at her.

"What did you do?" Jules gasped, pulling her arm from the girl. "What are you doing here?"

Finn began to breathe rapidly, almost hyperventilating, as she turned in a circle and took in the greenhouse around her. She rotated once completely and then her gaze found Henry and Jules again.

"How can that be?" Henry whispered, staring at her. "How can you be here?"

Finn looked at them seriously and began to shake her head. "I couldn't stay there. Not if there was anywhere else better to be. I just couldn't! It was terrible there, and I knew that you were from so far away. I saw you when you appeared out of nowhere. I been living on the streets o' New York as an orphan since our boat landed from my home in Cork, Ireland.

It was terrible. When you said you was going back to your home, I had to go too. I had to try. I didn't know if it would work, but I had to try."

She laughed and looked around her once more, then gazed back at Henry and Jules. "I can't thank you enough. This may be a strange new world, but it's already better than where I was!"

Henry finally tore his gaze from Finn and stared at Jules. "She ran away. She's a runaway. From 1849 in New York."

Jules was aghast. "I have no idea how we're going to explain this to Aunt Vianne. I have no idea what we're going to do with her."

Finn frowned and planted her hands on her hips. "Oy! I been living on me own on the streets o' New York City since I got off the boat, and it ain't been easy, but I managed. I'll manage again. Just point me to your town, and I'll make a go of it from there!"

Jules blinked in shock. "There's no way we're letting you run off on your own. How old are you?"

"I'm nine, goin' on ten." Finn said resolutely, as if that fixed everything.

"Nine?" Henry and Jules both said in unison.

Jules shook her head. "Well, that settles it. You're staying with us until we can find a good place for you to live."

It was Finn's turn to be surprised then. "Find a place… you mean, like an orphanage?"

Henry shook his head and reached his hand out to the small girl's shoulder. "No, like a home with a proper family who will look after you and take good care of you."

Finn's lower lip trembled. "Ain't no one been interested in doing anything like that for me."

"Well, you can't go out on your own. I don't care if you do have street smarts, you're nine. No nine year old should be living on the street." Jules stated flatly.

Finn could see that the discussion about her staying there was at an end. "Thank you, it's most kind o' you." She said quietly.

Henry and Jules nodded. "No trouble at all." Henry told her with a gentle smile.

"I think I better ask the same question you did when you first arrived in New York." Finn looked around and lowered her voice a little. "What year is it?"

"It's 2017." Henry answered her. "We're 168 years ahead of where you were living, and we're in upstate New York."

Finn swallowed. "We… we traveled through time?" She asked in a hollow voice.

Jules nodded and gave the sphere around her neck a cautious look. "I guess we did, though we didn't mean to. It was an accident."

Finn shook her head. "No it weren't. This is no accident. This is providence, that's what it were."

"We aren't sure what we did or how we did it." Jules told Finn the truth. "I think the best thing for all of us to do right now is to go in the house and have dinner and wait for Aunt Vianne."

"Who's that?" Finn asked curiously as she followed them out of the greenhouse.

"She's our aunt. We live with her." Henry explained. "I guess… I guess we're orphans too." He looked over at Jules, but she had her head turned. He knew it was hard for her to hear.

Finn stopped short when she saw the house looming up ahead of them. "That's not the house where you live!" She exclaimed in utter amazement.

Jules and Henry looked back over their shoulders at her. "It is. We've got a room for you; there's plenty of room."

She followed the two bigger children up the path to the house, and they took her wide-eyed and wonder-filled, up the stairs to the second level.

"There's another bedroom up here where you can stay while we figure things out." He opened the door to a good sized room that was all made up as a guest room. "This will be your room for now."

Finn stared at it. "A whole room all… all to meself?" She asked in a whisper as she took it in.

"Yes, we've each got our own rooms, and you will too, while you're here." Henry answered with a smile.

She shook her head. "I never woulda dreamed it."

Henry reached over and flipped the light on and began to walk across the room when Finn cried out again.

Jules and Henry both looked at her in astonishment. She was staring at the light on the ceiling. Jules laughed then and reached for the light switch, flipping it off, making Finn gasp again, and then flipping it back on once more.

Fascinated, Finn reached her own finger to the light switch and flipped it off and then back on again. "What is it? How does it work?"

"It's electricity." Henry answered, remembering their conversation in New York. "It's all over the house. Every room. It makes all of our appliances work too, when they're plugged in."

Finn could not get enough of the novelty of flipping the light switch. On. Off. On. Off.

Jules rolled her eyes, and she and Henry chuckled. Jules walked toward the bathroom that was in Finn's room. "You have your own bathroom in here, too."

Finn stopped playing with the light switch and followed them. "What? What is it?" She left the switch and followed Jules and Henry into the bathroom.

They showed her how it worked, and she played with the hot and cold water and flushed the toilet a couple of times, as well as flipping the light switch on and off over and again before she followed them back out.

Henry raised his brows and ran his hand over his stomach. "I'm famished. Are you hungry, Finn? Jules?"

"Yes." Jules answered, heading for the stairs.

"I'm always hungry." Finn replied with a small smile. She followed Henry and Jules, and together the three of them went down the stairs to the kitchen.

Jules and Henry heated up the dinner they had made for Vianne before they had inadvertently traveled through time, while Finn explored every part of the kitchen, studying the refrigerator and freezer, the toaster oven, the microwave, the coffee pot, and all of the other amenities that she could get her hands on.

"Aunt Vianne still isn't home yet." Jules told Henry, worriedly. "Is that normal for her? Does she do that very often?"

Henry shook his head. "No, she's usually really good about being here in the evenings. It's rare when she's gone, and when she is gone, she lets me know ahead of time that she won't be here."

Jules frowned and Henry tried to focus on their meal preparation.

"You were right!" Finn exclaimed happily as she examined the oven. "Everything is better here!"

Henry and Jules both smiled at the joy that was overtaking Finn as she checked out the world around her, completely mesmerized.

She finally stopped and sat with them at the table in the dining room when it was time to eat dinner. She seemed a little shy, and she explained that she'd never had such a fine meal in such a fine place before.

Jules gave the little girl a smile and tilted her head a bit. "How did you get your name Finn, if your given name is Fiona?"

Finn chuckled a little. "Me mum named me Fiona for my gran, but when I was wee, I couldn't say Fiona, all I could manage was Finn, and it stuck. I like it better now. Suits me fine."

She gave them each a curious look then. "What are you that you can travel in time and live in a place like this?" She asked, peering at them both.

"We're just kids. Just like you." Henry answered. "There's nothing special about us."

Finn leveled her gaze at him. "You brought me to this future from a time long past, well over a hundred years. There's something special about you."

Henry and Jules only shared a silent and questioning glance.

"What is this world like now?" Finn asked. "Save for the electricity." She had learned how to say it while she was going through the kitchen turning things on and off over and over again. Henry and Jules discovered that Finn was quite a fast learner.

"Well," answered Jules thoughtfully, "New York is one of the biggest cities in our country. The biggest cities are mostly on the coasts. There's New York and Boston, Philadelphia, and Washington D.C. where our leaders operate the country. That's all the east coast. Then on the west coast, there's Seattle, San Francisco, and Los Angeles."

Finn's eyes grew big. "I've heard talk o' San Francisco. Everyone is going there for the taking o' the gold."

"Well, they did, but it didn't last too long. There's still gold there, but it's all in technology." Henry replied with a lift of his brow.

"One of the biggest changes that you'll probably appreciate is that kids aren't allowed to work, not until they're fifteen or sixteen years old. All kids have to go to school. There are public schools all over the country where kids go to learn, and they go to school for free all the way up to the time they turn about eighteen. Then if they want to keep going to school, they go to a college or university and they have to pay for that." Henry told her thoughtfully.

Finn stared. "That's a mighty big change." She sighed with a shake of her head. "To think… I might even be able to go to school too! What a dream come true that would be. I'd love to learn how to write and read and do maths. I never thought I would have a chance to be in school."

"You might be home schooled with us here by my Aunt Vianne, but you'll definitely be educated. Nearly everyone is educated; it makes for a smarter country." Henry told Finn as they ate their dinner.

Finn was beaming at the idea. "I'm so glad I came to this time and place."

"Aren't you going to miss it in your own time at all?" Jules asked honestly, looking at her with intrigue.

Finn shook her head and grew quiet for a moment. "No. I was coming over from Cork with me family. We were trying to escape the potato famine. Me Mum and Da got cholera on the ship on the way over. T'was a ship by the name o' Swan. Like a swan on the water." She sighed and stared into the past. "Mum and Da passed away on the ship before we ever got to America. I pretended to be part of a big family that came in off the ship. They had so many young ones, I just blended into them. No one knew the difference coming through the docks. Once I was in the city, then I was on me own, and I had to figure it out. It were really hard at first, but that were six months ago, and I've gotten good at livin' on the streets now."

Jules and Henry were shocked and saddened. "That's so awful." Jules said in a whisper. "I'm so sorry."

Henry shook his head. "I can see why you left. You don't have to go back, if you don't want to. You're welcome to stay here with us until we find you a home of your own."

Finn seemed to snap out of her reverie and she looked back at them both. "Thank you. I'm most beholding to you."

She yawned then, trying to stifle it, and they all realized just how tired they were. They cleared away the dishes and put them in the dishwasher, much to Finn's delight, and then locked all the doors and headed upstairs to bed.

Finn was tickled to have a hot bath all her own, and her very own bed to sleep in. Jules helped her ready for bed and gave her one of her long t-shirts to wear as pajamas. Finn said she hadn't had a proper bed to sleep in for longer than she could remember.

Henry and Jules bid her goodnight and left the door open for her a crack. They said goodnight to one another and they each headed for their own beds, both of them exhausted and reeling from the unthinkable day they'd had.

The darkness and weariness combined to put them all into a deep sleep, and when the morning came, they were all rested and curious about what the day would bring.

Jules and Henry prepared breakfast for the three of them, with some help from Finn, and they talked about the most important issue at hand that morning.

"I looked in Aunt Vianne's room and she's not there. All of the outside doors on the house are still locked. She hasn't come home yet. I'm so worried about her." Henry said as he sliced fruit for them.

Jules frowned in consternation. "I don't know what we're going to do. We don't have anyone to turn to for help. What if something has happened to her?"

Henry stopped slicing, but didn't look up. "I was thinking about that."

"I was thinking about it, too. What if whoever came after my mom, went after Aunt Vianne? What if that's why she's been gone and hasn't been back yet?" Jules stood closer to him and spoke in a low voice while Finn set the dishes on the table.

"That's been on my mind since last night." Henry agreed with a quiet sigh. "There's something else, too."

"What's that?" Jules asked with a frown.

He looked up at her and glanced over her shoulder to make sure that Finn was out of earshot. "The necklace... the necklace that you have that belonged to our mom... Aunt Vianne had one almost exactly like it. What if her necklace took her somewhere like mom's did last night?"

Jules shook her head. "I'm not sure that the necklace was what took us, but it could be. We just don't have any answers right now. All we really have is questions, and now we have a nine year old girl to look after and no grown up around."

"I have a lot of questions too, and not to add to the pile of them, but take a look at this. Remember yesterday morning when you came into my room and I was reading?" He asked with a raised brow.

Jules nodded. "Yeah."

Henry reached for a book on the counter and handed it to her with a stoic face. "This is what I was reading."

Jules looked down at it as she took it into her hand. It was entitled, *'Emigration to New York in the 1800's'*. She stared at it and the image on it, an image that looked almost exactly like the place they had been to the night before, and where they had picked up Finn.

She looked back up at Henry sharply. "Wow! Do you think that has anything to do with why we went there?"

"How could it not? Our slip through time couldn't have been that random, could it? I've been studying this book the last couple of days as part of my history studies and homeschooling. Aunt Vianne has had me reading all kinds of books, which I love, but it just so happens that this is the current history book that I'm working through, then bam… all of a sudden that's where we wind up? Open it and look at the chapter. I haven't moved my bookmark since I closed it." He looked down at the book in her hands and she opened it.

The chapter he was reading was on Irish immigration in the mid 1800's. "Look at that paragraph." He said, pointing to the second page. On it was a list of ships that had sailed from Ireland to New York in the 1800's, and there under 1849, was a ship called the Swan. Jules gawked at the paragraph and was about to speak when Finn rounded the corner of the island and grinned at them. Some of her baby teeth were missing, but she could not have looked cuter to them.

Jules swiftly closed the book and tucked it behind her back, where Henry deftly slid it from her fingers and put it up on a high shelf. Finn either didn't see it or chose not to say anything about it.

"The table is ready." She beamed. She was a different looking girl, having been washed so thoroughly and slept so well in a comfortable bed. Henry had told her that it was a new bed and no one had ever slept in it before, which was true, and it delighted Finn to no end.

"Great! Thanks for helping. We'll be right in with breakfast. Go ahead and take your seat." Jules smiled at the girl, and Finn turned on the spot and almost bounced off to the nook where they were eating.

Jules turned to look at Henry. "We have got to figure this out, and we've got to do it fast. Something is going on here, and we need answers right away!"

"I know." He said quietly as he picked up the plate of fresh fruit he'd cut and Jules picked up the eggs and ham she'd cooked.

"I just don't know how to find the answers." He continued as they left the kitchen.

"Maybe there are answers in the greenhouse?" She suggested, almost pondering aloud.

"We searched the greenhouse yesterday. There wasn't anything but plants in there." He sighed.

They got to the table and both of them changed the topic of conversation. "We were thinking of trying to find some clothes and shoes for you that would fit you in this time and place." Jules said as they sat.

Finn looked down at her shabby, dirty, worn dress and oversized shoes. "I don't have any money, of course." She said, looking at each of them.

"We have some, at least enough to get you started, and then when Aunt Vianne returns, she can help us get you set." Henry told Finn.

"This is like a dream." Finn grinned as she dug into the hot breakfast.

"That's one way to put it." Jules said, glancing over at Henry.

They finished their breakfast and Finn was all too happy to do the dishes, loading them again into the dishwasher and loving the novelty of it.

Henry and Jules went to Vianne's office to try to see if there was anything in there that might give them a clue, but there was nothing. They left the office and went into the library, where they found Finn looking at the books set into the shelves.

"I can't wait to learn how to read and write. I'm going to read every book in this room. This must be every book in the world!" She grinned happily.

Henry shook his head. "Sadly, it's not even a drop in the bucket. I've read most of them twice, and most of the books in the library in town, too. We'll have you reading soon enough."

Finn shook her head. "I don't what it is that brought me here to be with you two, but I'm as glad as I can be that it happened. It's changing me whole life."

Henry and Jules shared a concerned look and a small smile. "We're both glad you're here too, Finn." Jules said, looking at the girl.

Finn tilted her head to one side and walked to where Henry and Jules were. "I been thinking about this trinket o' yours. This thing what took us out o' New York. Where else do you think it goes?"

She reached her hand up and held the globe in it, turning it and looking closely at it as she did. Jules and Henry both gasped and reached their hands to hers to pull it away from her, both of them crying out, "No!" at the same time.

There was a flash of light, and everything went black, and it stayed black for a long minute.

Chapter Four

~

The Time Palace

They found themselves encircled by a spacious area completely formed of a smooth white stone unlike any they had ever seen before. Though the darkness stayed all around the three children and seemed to go on forever, it slowly gave way to a soft glow of silvery blue light that seemed to be emanating from the white stone of the courtyard.

The glowing stone stretched out from where they stood to the edge of the court where columns rose, towering four times the height of Jules; each one wound with a wandering vine upon which strange flowers grew.

All three of them looked around slowly and stared, trying to take it all in. Beyond the courtyard was a great building made of the same glowing white stone and glass that looked as if it might be crystal, refracting light into prismatic colors. The structure was palatial, with varying levels at different heights, some flat walls, some rounded walls, rows of columns here and there connecting different parts of it together, and all of it looking completely otherworldly.

They were silent, but they all reached for each other's hands. The quietness around them was broken by the sound of a shuffling noise; like the soft thud of metal landing on something solid.

It was then that they noticed a winding path leading from the courtyard where they were standing, toward the massive edifice before them.

As they gazed at the path and the origin of the dull clunking that thumped closer and closer, a small machine came into view. It was just a little taller than Jules' knee. All three of them stared at it in breathless silence.

Coming around the bend in the path toward them was an animal made entirely of metal. It was waddling on its two thick hind legs, it had a paunch belly, and two small arms with claws at the ends. Its face was small, with a short snout and two big dark mechanical eyes. Atop its head were two ears perked up, and behind it was a tail that was thick close to its body and narrowed as it reached a point two feet out behind the creature.

"Is that a dragon?" Jules whispered in utter disbelief. "A little… metal dragon?"

The scales of the small dragon were layers of metal that looked as if they were carefully crafted and delicately placed, shifting as the creature moved, almost as if it was all a real skin fitted on it.

The children stood stock still and the miniature dragon gradually reached them, stopping a few feet before them and looking up at them with a friendly smile.

"Welcome to the Time Palace." It said in a light and slightly high tone. "I'm Sprocket. May I ask who you are?"

Jules blinked in utter shock at the little machine that was speaking to her. "This has got to be a dream." She said almost under her breath. The little dragon waited, watching her.

Straightening herself, she planted her hands on her hips and lifted her chin a little. "We're the Starlings of Ramblewood." She announced, wondering if any of it was real.

The little dragon nodded. "That's what I thought."

"What are you?" Henry asked, peering closely at it, and leaning over slightly, planting his hands on his knees as he examined the creature curiously.

Sprocket beamed a little. "I'm a mechanimal."

Jules lowered one brow and raised the other quizzically. "You look like a baby dragon."

Sprocket nodded and pressed his petite claws together as if he was clasping hands. "I am a dragon today, because I'm on duty. I can change shape to resemble almost any animal."

"Are you alive?" Finn frowned slightly, tilting her head at an angle as she tried to work out in her mind just what he was.

He shook his head, his big dark eyes meeting her gaze. "No. I'm all machine, but I can communicate and problem solve. Also, I'm a handy assistant."

Jules shook her head slowly and then looked up at the darkness that completely enveloped them, save for the structure where they were standing. There were brilliant specks of light all over the darkness; some bigger than others, some smaller, many in different colors; white, blue, red, green, brown, and on and on.

"Where are we? This looks like space." She said quietly, taking it all in.

Sprocket nodded. "You are correct, you are in space. You are from Earth, and we are not very far away from earth. You can see it from just over here." He waddled away from them and they shared a stunned look before tentatively following after him toward the edge of the courtyard.

There was a glowing stone banister that stretched the entire perimeter of the courtyard. They stopped and looked over the edge of it. There was nothing beneath them but space, and at a fair distance, the

Earth. Their home planet looked a little closer than the full moon at night to their homes.

All three of the children gasped and gaped. Henry set his hands upon the banister, but Finn reached for Jules hand and held it tightly.

"Where did you say we are?" Jules whispered, her eyes wide, locked on the planet where she had always lived.

"You're at the Time Palace. The Empress has sent for you, that's why you're here." Sprocket told her kindly.

She turned and frowned down at him. "What is the Time Palace? Who is the Empress? How do you know who we are?"

Sprocket waved a claw at them to follow him and he spoke as he shuffled away from them. "The Time Palace is where all time in the known universe is monitored. They don't keep it here, they just look after it, and when something goes wrong at any time, they fix it." He began. "The Time Empress oversees all of it. She's quite powerful. She could tell you how she knows who you are."

Henry skipped a step ahead to catch up with Sprocket. "You said 'they'… who were you talking about?"

Sprocket hesitated and glanced up at him, then kept heading toward the palace. "I shouldn't try to explain more. I must leave that to the Empress. She's waiting to see you."

"How did we get here?" Jules asked, hurrying to catch up to Sprocket and Henry, with Finn still holding tightly to her hand.

Sprocket gave her an uncertain glance. "I'm not sure that I can-" he began, but Jules gave him a pleading look.

"You must tell us! This has been the craziest day ever, and the strangest things keep happening! We just want to know what's going on!" She reached her hand out to touch him and stop him.

Sprocket paused in his short step and turned toward her for a moment. "It's that piece you're wearing around your neck on the chain. That's how you got here, that and the Empress, because she wanted you here. Now, I can't say anything else. We must go see her. You can ask her all of your questions."

He waved his small metal claw at them again and they followed him, staring at the Time Palace as they came to a great arched door made of shimmering crystal, scattering prisms in every color from it that seemed to shift and dance with every step the children took toward it.

The doors opened just as Sprocket and the children reached them, without being touched at all. They swept inward, parting from each other, and the company entered the palace without a word.

They walked quietly down a great hall filled with sculpted arches that reached up loftily overhead, and touched each other at the top of the ceiling, which looked as much like a starry night sky as the infinite space outside did.

Sprocket waddled down a good distance of the hall, passing more arches and doors that led to other mysterious parts of the palace, and finally he came to a stop at the end of the hall, where two more arched double doors stood closed. They were made of the same white stone as the rest of the palace, and they too glowed with the same silvery blue light.

The little mechanimal reached his claw forward and tapped it gently on the stone. A hollow beat sounded, and a moment later, both of the doors opened inward.

They stepped into a great round room with a dome ceiling. At the center of the dome was a circle framed by glistening crystals in varying shades of blue, green, purple, turquoise, rose, and some slight amber.

Falling through the hole just around the edge of it, was a silvery looking stream that seemed as though it might have been water, but it was finer, like streaming strands that glistened and shone, made of something none of them had ever seen. Upon closer examination, one could see that within the streams there were strange looking symbols that fell in randomly alternating places, one symbol after another, after another, and then suddenly stopping and flowing in another part of the falls. The stream fell silently into a smooth crystal pool that was precisely the same circumference as the crystal circle in the ceiling above it. The stream looked as if it disappeared as it entered the pool; never filling it or overflowing it.

Somehow, at the center of the falls where the hole in the ceiling was, the stream was hollow; the mysterious flow only fell exactly at the edge of the circle, and nothing was inside of it.

Through the hole in the domed ceiling, the children could see space outside of the Time Palace; stars, nebulas, galaxies, and an expanse of the universe so vast that it was endless. The same view was shown through several tall oval looking windows that spanned most of the room. They weren't quite windows, as much as they were openings between what looked like tree trunks whose roots and branches reached out to each other, creating the spaces between them that looked like windows to the universe.

There was a very natural feel to room. The almost-trees and almost-water in the fall, as well as the crystals that made up so much of what they were looking at; jagged around the hole in the ceiling, but smoothed over the rest of the dome and walls; all of it made the place feel as if it were a mystical cousin of the earth in some way.

The children stared at everything in silence, fascinated and curious, fearful and uncertain, all at once.

Standing near the strange glowing falls was a woman. She had long white hair with wavy curls at the ends of it reaching far past her waist, violet eyes, and pale skin. She was the tallest woman any of them had ever seen, taller than a human woman, but resembling a human in every way, save for her eyes, her height, and the willowy look about her that gave her an extremely graceful sort of air. Her lavender gown was draped lightly on her, and seemed to flow out behind her, giving the impression that it might be moving in some gentle wave of water or breeze, though there was none around her.

She was watching them, regarding them, with her long, slender hands folded lightly before her.

Finn squeezed Jules' hand tighter. "I'm scared." She whispered. Jules gave her hand a squeeze back, but she kept her eyes on the Time Empress before her.

A clinking noise caught their attention and the children turned to see Sprocket beside them. His form began to shift, and his tiny dragon wings and tail started to fold into his back. His pointy ears whirred and spun, and his snout sunk back into his face. A few moments later, as he changed before their eyes, Sprocket took on the form of a teddy bear, and when he was completely finished in his transition, the teddy bear softly stepped up to Finn and took her other hand.

She accepted his paw slowly and cautiously, her wide-eyed gaze of wonder steady on him. He looked up at her and gave her a sweet teddy bear smile, and she smiled back at him.

The Time Palace

On the far wall of the room, opposite the windows, were seven full head to toe silvery bluish glowing holograms of people. Each of them appeared to be moving slightly; breathing, blinking, looking around subtly, as if they might be watching what was going on in the room.

Though Henry took a good look at them, Jules only glanced at them and then turned her attention back to the Empress, who was watching them; her expression unreadable.

She took a few steps toward them, and spoke. Her voice was calm and yet strong; powerful without being loud, and somehow commanding yet patient.

"You are the Starling children, or at least, two of you are." She began, looking at each one of them for a lingering moment.

"We are." Jules answered, her chin raised again confidently, though she felt no real confidence in herself in that place and at that moment. "This is our… our friend, Finn." She didn't look away from the Empress as she introduced the young girl, but instead she kept her eyes on the woman.

"I am the Time Empress, and you are in the Time Palace, as you are now aware." The Empress stated, and Jules saw a strange light in her violet eyes. "I am displeased that you are here."

"We didn't come here on purpose." Henry replied, miffed that they were being scolded for being in a place where they hadn't intended to be.

"No, you didn't." The Empress continued. "I brought you here out of necessity. You weren't supposed to come here until much later."

Jules and Henry blinked in surprise and shared a glance of confusion with one another before looking back at her.

The Empress looked at Sprocket then. "Sprocket, please take Henry to the library and Finn to the Moon

Garden. I'll send for them when it's time for them to leave."

Jules shook her head and held fast to Finn's hand. "They stay with me. We don't know where we are, and we're not going to be separated. We don't even know why we're here."

The Empress walked toward them and stood just a few feet from Jules. "None of you have a choice. I will not discuss what you and I will be talking about in front of them, they are too young. They will leave and you and I will talk, and when we are finished talking, you will all be sent home together."

Jules studied the woman's face and eyes and realized that the woman was right. She could see that they had no choice.

"Fine, but I want to be sure they'll be safe; that we'll all be safe." Jules planted her hands on her hips firmly.

The Empress nodded faintly. "You could be in no safer place; of that, I can assure you."

With a sigh of resignation, Jules let go of Finn's hand and looked deeply into Henry's eyes. "Be careful. I'll be here if you need anything."

He nodded and took Finn's hand in his, giving his sister one last look over his shoulder as he followed teddy bear Sprocket out of the large room.

When the doors closed behind them, leaving Jules alone with the Empress, Jules turned to face the woman and she left her hands on hips. "Who are you, why are we here, where are we, and what is this place?"

She thought she'd start with the simple questions and go from there. Her mind was flooded with many more questions that she was determined to have answered.

The Empress looked into her eyes and Jules felt as if she was staring into the vast expanse of the universe, rather than at a person.

Sprocket took Henry and Finn down the long hall and then turned down a corridor that was only slightly smaller than the main hall in which they'd been. They walked a good distance, and finally the mechanimal stopped before a large and intricately carved set of wooden doors that reached from floor to ceiling. He pressed his paw on one of them, and they both opened.

He waved them in and they stepped into the biggest room that Henry or indeed Finn, had ever been in. It was a massive library. It extended upward three stories and was all wide open, going back from the corner where they stood for as far as they could see, and much further than they couldn't see.

There was a moment of silence, and then a rustling noise sounded in the rows and rows of towering bookshelves before them. The rows filled the main floor, and all along the walls around the massive space, from the ground to the arched ceiling, were shelves lined with books of every color and shape, of every size, and of every age.

"I'm in heaven. I've died and gone to heaven." Henry whispered as his wide eyes took in everything around him.

Sprocket shook his head, and the rustling noise in the rows grew louder, seeming to move closer to them. "You aren't dead. This is the Universal Library. I'm leaving you with Rastaban. You'll be safe with him."

"Rasta... what?" Henry asked, his brow furrowing slightly as he finally tore his eyes from the countless books before him and looked down at the little teddy bear.

"Rastaban." Came a deep and calm sounding voice. It resonated, filling all of the area around them, surrounding them, reverberating inside them.

All three of them turned and looked up to find an enormous caterpillar or worm-like creature gazing down at them. Finn screamed, but not much sound came out. She was terrified. The teddy bear patted her hand and gave it a gentle squeeze. Henry could only stare. The creature regarded them.

He was more than twice the height of Henry, and his body was so wide that it nearly filled the row of books from which he had come. Henry saw that the worm's body stretched far back down the row, until he couldn't even see it anymore. The body had sections, like a worm, but each one was a different color; some of the colors repeated, but most of them were entirely individual from every other color that could be seen.

On top of the creature's body, all along his back and up to the top of his head, was a feathery looking colorful fringe; it looked silky soft, and as the caterpillar-worm moved ever so slightly, the fringe wavered gently. It varied in color as much as his body did. All along the bottom of him there were feet; one row on each side, and several of them were clutching books, as far down the length of him as Henry could see.

Rastaban had a face, almost resembling a human, with two eyes and a nose, with cheeks and a mouth, and he even had very fine soft white whiskers that drifted down over his mouth and chin. His eyes were dark, and they were set upon his visitors.

"What can I do for you?" He asked patiently, not seeming to mind their scrutiny of him.

Sprocket spoke up. "I am Sprocket. The Empress sent me to bring young Henry to the library. He is to stay here until he is summoned back to her."

"Then he shall stay with me." Rastaban answered. "Will you and this young girl be staying as well?"

Henry was surprised that Rastaban did not know who Sprocket was, and the question of why that might be was on his mind for a moment as the little mechanimal replied to the great creature.

"We must go to the Moon Garden. Thank you for taking Henry." Sprocket turned then and left with Finn close beside him.

Henry realized that he was staring and his good manners bit at him. He blinked and looked around the library for a moment before speaking to Rastaban again.

"I didn't know that there would be a library here." He began, uncertain of what to say. He'd never spoken to such a creature before.

"There is, and it is the biggest library in the universe, for it holds every book that has ever been made, from every world, and it is constantly growing. There is nothing that is written that is not in this library." Rastaban answered.

Henry was dumbfounded. "All things written? For how long?" He asked, unable to stop from letting his eyes leave the worm and drift over the endless rows of books before them.

"All things, for all time." Rastaban answered. "I am the librarian. I take care of all of it. I read everything here, and the more I read, the longer I grow."

Henry's mouth fell open as he began to understand just how long the worm was. Its body went the full length of the row he'd come out of to greet them at the door, and then it wound back into the row behind that, and then the row behind that, and it seemed to go on forever.

"What a treasure!" he gasped, his green eyes glazing over. He turned back to his host then. "What are you?" He asked, willing himself not to stare.

"I'm a bookworm." Rastaban laughed, and the deep sound echoed like giant brass cathedral bells throughout the gigantic hall.

A smile cracked at the corner's of Henry's mouth. Despite the strangeness of all of it, he knew that he liked the bookworm then and there, and he felt excitement bubbling up in him, along with an endless explosion of questions.

Sprocket and Finn went down a few more halls and stepped out of a pair of crystal doors. The doors opened onto a small courtyard, similar to the one that the children had first landed on. There were pillars and vines, glowing bluish white stone, and there was much more in the little courtyard than there had been in the bigger one they'd seen when they arrived.

At the center of the circle of the court was a shallow pool, filled with translucent turquoise colored water, and it glinted on the top with the brilliance of the stars that were nearest to the Time Palace. There was a bench beside the pool, and Sprocket took Finn to it, sitting on it with her.

Around them was a carefully manicured garden, with bushes and potted trees, and the strangest flowers that Finn had ever seen. The ones she liked best looked like dark purple violets, but there were white stars of different sizes and shapes on the flower petals, that seemed to be moving slowly over them.

"Sprocket?" Finn asked, looking over at him when she had spied most of the garden and the pool.

The teddy bear looked at her. "Yes?"

"Thank you for staying with me." She told him in a quiet voice. "My name's Finn."

He smiled his friendly bear smile at her, and his dark eyes shone. "Sometimes in strange places, we can find new and good friends. I am your friend, Finn. I will take care of you."

She reached her arm around his small shoulders and hugged him.

Henry slipped his hands into his pants pockets and tilted his head a little as he looked at the bookworm. "You're truly fascinating. Where do you come from? How did you get your name? I think the name Rastaban is from one of the stars in the Draco or dragon constellation. Are you named after that star?" He was trying to hold all of his questions at bay, or at least to stem the stream of some of them.

Rastaban chuckled and gave him a nod, and as he moved his great head, the fringe on him swayed and danced. "Such a curious lad. That's so good. Curiosity will help you all of your life. Ask about everything, always." He began. Then a faraway look came into his eyes. "I'm from a planet that was very small, and it no longer exists. It was hit by a comet a millennia ago, and it was destroyed, but by then I was already here at the palace." He sighed a little and then looked back at Henry. "I am impressed that you know about the star in the Draco constellation. I am named for that star. Now, how did you come to be here, and who are you?"

Henry grinned at the giant bookworm. "I'm Henry Starling. I'm from Earth. I'm not really sure how we came to be here. I'm here with my sister Jules and our new friend Finn." He saw such compassion in the old worm's eyes that he felt he could confide in him. "It's going to sound as if we've lost our minds, but the truth is, I think we time traveled, and then somehow we did it again to come here. I've been pondering this since we arrived here. Are we in the future here? Is the Time Palace in the future?"

Rastaban regarded him with a mixture of wisdom and delight. "You did not time travel when you came here. The Time Palace is free of time; they monitor it here, the Time Guild Keepers, but time does not pass here the way that it does in other places. When you return to Earth, you will be returning to the same time and place that you left."

The great worm was quiet a moment and then his deep voice spoke more softly. "You are the son of one of the Starling sisters, is that correct?"

Henry nodded. "Yes, only… I've just found out the truth about that, too. I've lived with my Aunt Vianne all these years, and I've only just discovered that my mother, Marleigh Starling, was alive all my life. I was told she had passed away when I was a baby. I also just found out that I have a sister; Jules. It's been really confusing." He stopped short then and stared at Rastaban, agape. "Wait, how do you know them?" He was positively thunderstruck.

Rastaban gave him a kindly smile. "The Starling sisters are friends of mine. I've known them since they were young. It is not common knowledge that there are children, either Vianne's or Marleigh's, though I did suspect it for some time. How wise it was of them to keep you and your sister separated. That clever deception does not surprise me, coming from those two. It is indeed an honor to meet you, Henry Starling. A rare and wonderful honor."

Henry felt his heart tug. "Thank you. I'm sorry to tell you, but Marleigh was killed recently, though I don't know how or by whom, and Vianne has gone missing since then."

Rastaban shook his head and his fringe waved with the movement. "I'm so terribly sorry to hear that. I think a great deal of them both."

Henry frowned and crossed his arms over his chest. His mind was a flurry of questions, and more were blossoming within him with each passing second. "How could you possibly know them? Did they come here? What were they doing here? What do they have to do with this place? Do you know why my sister and I were brought here? Why did Jules and I need to be separated?"

The old bookworm was quiet for a moment. "My goodness you have so many questions. The answers to all of those are held within one story, and it's quite a long story, Henry."

"Oh please, tell me! I need to know!" Henry implored emphatically.

Rastaban and Henry
In the Time Palace Library

Jules stood before the Empress, waiting for some kind of explanation that might begin to answer all of the questions whirring through her mind.

The Empress gazed at her for a long moment, and finally spoke. Her voice was as calm and even as it had been when they'd first arrived. "The Time Palace is where all time in the universe is monitored. This is no planet or artificially constructed station in space, but rather an organic and living edifice; the entire palace that you see and everything in it and on it is alive in one way or another. It is anchored by the magnetic force of the Sentinels. The Sentinels are four bright stars which exist at a slight distance from this place, all set at even intervals. Everything within the area of the Sentinels is part of the Time Palace, including the magnetic field which holds the structure in place."

She turned and lifted her graceful hand, her long thin fingers indicating all seven of the holograms lining the far wall. "These are the members of the Time Guild Keepers, and I am on the council of keepers. I oversee every aspect of the Time Palace and all that is done here, and done in the name of the palace."

Jules walked to the holograms and studied them in fascination. Beside the translucent shimmering image of the Empress was a hologram of a warrior who looked Asian. He was strong and solemn; outfitted in a warrior's armor. It was clear that he was powerful without trying to show it. Beneath his shifting figure was a plaque that read, 'Shen'.

Walking along the row, Jules looked at each of them. There was Andrei, who had the appearance of an Italian businessman, with handsome features and wavy dark hair streaked with silver, and deep dark eyes. Meri, who also looked as if she was from the Mediterranean region, with short, cropped, mahogany hair around her head like a pixie, and olive skin like Jules'. She reminded Jules of Joan of Arc. She seemed to have great strength, and a smile just at the corner of her mouth.

Kaspar was tall and regal looking, with wide shoulders and a long, drawn face. His black hair had given way to much silver over his head and through the trimmed beard on his face. His eyes were onyx, and his mouth was a thin line. He had an austere presence about him that Jules found somewhat intimidating.

Beside Kaspar was Tzafrir, who was tall and muscular, with a squared jaw set firmly, as if there was nothing that could defeat him. His skin was dark, he had no hair, and his chocolate brown eyes looked as though they shone with pride and courage. His stance, though only a hologram, also exuded bravery. Jules wondered if he was from Africa or someplace like it. He wore a thin beige and dark brown tunic over cream colored pants, with a leather belt that held a silver sword. She thought that he might be a desert warrior.

Last was Armati. The woman's image was tall, even a little taller than Tzafrir beside her, and she was all muscle; toned and strong, fit and fair. Her skin was light, her hair hung about her shoulders and back to her waist in thick, blonde waves. She wore a white and gold bodice, and a short white skirt that lay in folds high on her legs. On her head was a golden crown and she carried a silver and golden sword. Her bright blue eyes shone with a fire from deep within. She was mighty, and it filled Jules with awe to see her image.

"These are the Time Guild Keepers?" Jules asked, giving them one more look before she turned back to the Empress.

The Empress nodded. "They are. They are from different parts of the universe; some from earth, others of them like me, are from other planets."

She walked slowly over to the streaming fall that slid from the ceiling into the pool. "There are Time Guardians who work for the Guild Keepers here at the palace. Your mother and aunt are both Time Guardians, or they were. They were the finest that we had."

Jules was astounded. She found her voice after a minute, though her throat felt dry as she spoke. "What does a Time Guardian do?"

The Empress turned and looked over her shoulder at her. "You see these streams before us, falling into the pool. They are strands of time. Each one has its own signature. Time passes differently all over the universe. It doesn't actually exist, but it is used as a means of measurement. Sometimes things go wrong with time, and that's when we have a guardian travel to correct it. One of the recent things that has gone wrong with time is that we have discovered that there is a great amount of it being stolen. Your mother and your aunt were the best of all the guardians, and they were tracking the pirates who were responsible for stealing the time that was missing. We believe that the Starlings were on the verge of catching them."

Jules dropped her hands to her side. "Pirates? You must be kidding."

One look from the Empress told her that she was being completely serious. "Time pirates."

"How does someone steal time?" Jules asked with a doubtful brow low over her eye.

The Empress turned and gazed into the ever-flowing stream of time strands before her. "Perhaps you've experienced the loss of time, when you feel like it's only been a few minutes, but several minutes or hours have passed, and you might say, 'where did the time go'. There are many ways that time is taken, but most often when you feel you have lost it somehow, it's because time was stolen from you, and you didn't realize it. The Time Guardians protect time, they keep it safe, they make sure it's not tampered with or changed, or stolen. When it is, they go and correct it." She turned and looked back at Jules then. "Just as there are those who would protect it, there are also those who would abuse and use it, or steal it, as has been happening constantly of late."

Jules drew in a deep breath. "Well I hate to be the one to break it to you, but my mother Marleigh was just killed, and now my Aunt Vianne has gone missing. Do you think it was the time pirates who did it?" Jules felt for the first time since her mother had disappeared that she might actually get a real answer.

The Empress' face grew sorrowful. "I am aware of it, and it was I who sent the officer to your home to tell you about your mother's death. I am truly dismayed about that, but I promise you that we will search for your aunt until we find her."

"What about the pirates?" Jules pressed further. "Is anyone going to go after them? Are there other guardians stopping them?"

The Empress shook her head, and her silvery white hair moved delicately behind her shoulders. "You do not need to know everything right now. In fact, you never should have been here until you turned sixteen. You know far more at this moment than you should at all. Now, give me the Cerellus."

Jules blinked. "The what?"

The Empress grew serious. "That pendant around your neck. That is what makes your time travel possible. It's called a Cerellus, and you have no business wearing it, at least not until you are of age, and that's a long while from now. Hand it over to me, and I will keep it safe until it is time to give it to you."

Jules felt a fire kindle and grow deep inside of her, and she knew that it might be dangerous; she knew that the Empress was no one to trifle with, but she was determined to stand her ground. "I will not give it to you. This was my mother's, and I don't have much left of her. I'm keeping it."

The Empress gazed at her thoughtfully and said nothing at first, but then she looked away and nodded. "I understand. Keep it then, but do not use it under any circumstance. I will give you this box to safeguard it. Place it in here, and do not ever put it on or touch it until I have summoned you back here when you are sixteen."

With that, the Empress waved her hand and a small light blue box appeared in her other hand. It was a beautiful box, with a translucent aquamarine stone on top of it, at the center. She handed the box to Jules, and the girl took it and examined it.

"Thank you." She replied, not saying one way or the other that she would use it. She hadn't made up her mind at all as to what she was going to do with the Cerellus pendant around her neck, and she wasn't going to make any promises while she was still uncertain.

"It is time for you to leave." The Empress said in her soft voice. She waved her hand again, and a moment later the doors opened, and Sprocket the teddy bear came in with Finn and Henry.

"Now, you three go back to Ramblewood and stay there. I shall send someone to look after you until your aunt is found. In the meantime, be sure you remember what I told you, Jules." She gave the young girl a stern look, and Jules nodded.

An instant later, all three of them were standing on the front porch of the house at Ramblewood, and it was as if they had never left, except for one thing.

Finn squealed. "Sprocket!" She exclaimed in happy surprise. The little bear rotated its metal head and looked up at her.

"It was real…" Henry said quietly, reaching his hand carefully to the pocket on the front of his shirt and giving it a gentle touch.

Jules looked down at the blue box in her hand. "It looks like it was real, though I can't honestly believe it."

The light around them began to fade and black smoke seemed to come from nowhere, billowing around them. They looked around in fright, crying out for one another as they grasped at each other's hands. The black cloud grew thicker, and the children coughed a few times, and then fell silently to the porch, asleep.

Chapter Five

~

The Gypsy Windlass

Henry opened his eyes and looked around. He was laying on a thick, comfortable bed with a short, well crafted and carved wooden railing around it. Looking over the railing, he saw that what he was resting on was a very fine cot far above the floor, and it was one of four beds in a good sized cabin. The beds were affixed to the wall and closed up flush against the wall when unused, or opened outward for use when needed. There was another exceptional cot below him where Finn lay asleep, and on the adjacent wall were two more cots; the higher of them folded up and secured to the wall, while the lower cot was opened, and Jules was sleeping on it.

He looked about the cabin in amazement. It was as luxurious a room as he had ever seen. There was a door open that led to a bathroom where he could see a shower, toilet, and sink with a mirror. There was a small sofa in one corner, and an armchair next to it, and along the wall above the sofa were bookshelves lined with books, held in by a low bar that spanned the length of each shelf. Beside the fireplace was a small square table with a kettle and a tray, arranged with four teacups, a container of teas, and a covered crystal dish of biscuits.

Henry crawled over the short railing around the bed and quietly lowered himself to the floor. He walked over to a set of double doors that opened into a shallow walk-in closet. There were three sides to it, and all three sides were filled with clothes that he could see in an instant were there for Jules, Finn, and himself. There were shoes in a rack along the floor, and a short set of drawers on each of the three walls, each drawer filled with folded clothes for them.

He walked into the small bathroom and saw three hooks on the back of the door, and on each hook was a robe and a pair of slippers that were held there with a satin string and clips.

Giving his reflection in the mirror a curious look, he left the bathroom and frowned. He went to Jules and reached his hand out to her to wake her. At his gentle pushes, her eyes flew open and she sat up, looking wildly around them.

"Henry! What happened? Where are we?" She gasped, blinking in confusion at their surroundings.

He spoke in a low voice. "I don't know. I just woke up myself. So far all I know is that we are in a cabin. There's a bathroom and a closet, and it looks as if this whole place was designed with the three of us in mind. There are even clothes and shoes for us in the closet, and robes in the bathroom. Someone was planning on us being here. Wherever here is." He frowned and looked around again.

Jules sat up and looked at the bed she had been sleeping in. Her hand moved over the softest sheets she'd ever felt, and the fluffy pillow where she'd been dreaming. She touched the polished railing that edged her cot. "What in the world is going on? What is this place?"

Henry cocked his head to one side. "If I was going to guess, I'd say this is a cabin on some kind of transportation vessel, like a train or a boat. It's very nice and there is some space, but you can see that it's designed to be compact, and to fit four people in here comfortably. That's how cabins are. This isn't a bedroom, at least not like one you'd see in a house."

"We were at the house, and then there was a black cloud of... something. It wasn't smoke. I don't know what it was. Then I fell asleep, and I don't remember anything until waking up just now. Do you remember anything? Do you know how we got here?" Jules asked, turning her eyes to her brother.

He shook his head. "I don't. It was the same for me; one minute we were at Ramblewood, and the next, I woke up here in this cabin."

Jules pushed herself up off of the bed. "Well, at least we're all together." She went to Finn's bed, beneath Henry's cot, and woke the girl.

"Do you think we're prisoners?" Henry asked, rising and walking to the wood paneling around the room. "If we are, this is a very fine prison. I've never been in a room so luxurious before."

Finn gasped and reached for Jules, holding her arm tightly as she looked around. "Where are we?" She asked, her eyes wide and her voice on edge.

"We're trying to figure that out." Jules answered, standing up straight. Finn got out of the bed and then turned to look at it appreciatively.

"I never slept anywhere so nice as that spot." She said wistfully.

"Me neither." Henry admitted with a little smile. "And it's pretty comfortable at Aunt Vianne's."

Finn stopped short and held her hands to the railing of Henry's bed near her head. She looked at the other two anxiously. "We're on a ship."

Henry and Jules looked back at her in astonishment. "A ship?" asked Jules. "How do you know that?"

Finn looked around the room. "Can't you feel that sway? I know it's just a little, but we're not on steady ground. I was on a ship for a long time on the crossing from Cork to America. I know the feel of a ship. We're on a ship."

Jules planted her hands on her hips and narrowed her eyes as she examined their new quarters. "You know, the Time Empress said that she was going to send someone to look after us. Do you suppose that wherever we are now, it's with whoever it is that will be taking care of us?" She asked suspiciously.

Just then there was the soft clang of a metallic sounding knock at the door. Each of the children looked at one another, and Henry moved to open the door carefully, pulling it inward toward him.

A small metal dog stood before them. It wagged its tail and jumped up on its hind legs, pawing at them a little with its front feet, its dark eyes shining.

"Sprocket?" Finn asked in surprise, going to the creature. "You're a dog?"

"Yes!" he answered, and the children recognized the sound of his voice right away. "I'm a companion right now." He seemed pleased about it.

"Sprocket, where are we?" Jules asked, looking down at him.

He wagged his rear end and rubbed his head against Finn's leg. "You're on the Gypsy Windlass." He answered.

"I knew we was on a ship." Finn stated with certainty.

"You must come with me." Sprocket said, looking at them.

"Are we safe?" Jules peeked out of the doorway and found a long passageway made of wood, with a narrow thick red carpet stretching the length of it, but not fully covering the width of the floor.

"You are quite safe." Sprocket answered, trotting out into the hall, heading toward the shorter end of it where there was another doorway that was open. He looked back over his shoulder. "Come along!" He barked happily at them.

The three of them shared an uncertain look, and then with sighs of resignation, they followed the little mechanimal down the hall and up two flights of stairs.

They stepped out onto the main deck, and saw that they were on a massive ship, though it was designed in a way that they could never have imagined.

It had a beautiful light wood deck, polished and gleaming, and in the center of the deck was a wide circular brass pillar that rose heavenward, and around the pillar was an enormous cream colored balloon, as round as a globe. At the greatest circumference of the balloon was a sizeable walking platform where a guardhouse stood. There were ladders that led up to the platform and guardhouse, and from that point, there were ladders that led up to the top of the balloon. It was the strangest and greatest thing that any of the children had ever seen. There was a good deal more about the ship to see, but Jules was most concerned with where they were, rather than what the vessel they stood upon looked like.

The ship was floating on water inside an enormous cave. The mouth of the cave was rimmed with thick and lush greenery, from flowers and bushes to great vines. It was all shrouded on the outside of the cave by a massive waterfall that was dense enough to hide the ship, but with the sunlight on the other side, the children could see through it that there was an ocean beyond the waterfall.

Jules and Henry were looking around at the cave and the ship, but Finn was looking immediately around them. She curled her small hand into a fist, her dark eyes leveled on a group of people who had begun to gather around them.

Henry and Jules shifted their gazes to the crowd. There were men and women of many ages and races around them, all of them looking on at the children with kind and pleasant faces.

Jules felt her heart begin to pound. Henry took her hand and Finn's in his, and held fast to them. Sprocket bounded around happily in the space between them and the people who encircled them.

One of them stepped forward from the group. He was a tall, broad-shouldered man with wavy black hair, cropped at his neck and longer on top of his head, with sky blue eyes and a closely trimmed black beard and moustache just barely covering his squared jaw and narrow cheeks.

"Welcome aboard the Gypsy Windlass." He called out in a robust voice. "I'm Captain Kadian Aragon." He turned and looked over his right shoulder at the man who was standing beside him. "This is my first mate, August Holt."

August was slightly smaller than the strapping Captain, a few inches shorter, with tousled looking dark brown hair around his head and a fuller, thicker beard and moustache. August gave them a nod of greeting.

"Who are you and what are we doing here?" Jules demanded, crossing her arms over her chest.

The corner of the Captain's mouth lifted slightly, as if he was bemused somewhat, but holding it back. He spoke to them with an earnest tone. "We are enemies of the time pirates. Now, you know who we are, perhaps you ought to tell us who you are."

Henry frowned sharply. "You brought us here and you don't know who we are? Do you randomly abduct children?"

Jules lifted her chin and spoke with a clear voice. "We're the Starlings of Ramblewood." She announced.

Captain Aragon turned and looked at August intently, and August lifted an eyebrow and pressed his lips together into a thin line.

The Captain turned then and took a few steps toward the children. He was dressed in black, from his loose fitting shirt with a V neck that wasn't quite laced closed, to his snug black pants that tucked into his black leather boots, reaching just under his knees. He casually rested his left hand on the elegantly crafted and bejeweled hilt of a long silver cutlass that hung off of his belt. On his other hip lay a black leather holster wherein was nestled a long barreled automatic steel pistol.

"We do not abduct children, save for perhaps this one time." He eyed them with interest. "I suspected that you might be the Starlings, and when we learned that you were, we knew that we must talk with you." The Captain eyed Henry, and Jules saw that there was a strange glint in his eyes.

"What do you need us for? We're only children!" Henry demanded, glaring up at the Captain.

Captain Aragon took his time answering, looking at each of them in turn. He leaned forward a little as he spoke. "My crew and I are about to embark upon a quest to go find the Commodore of the time pirates. I am certain that it was he who captured Vianne, and killed Marleigh."

Henry and Jules were stunned at the mention of their mother and aunt by the Captain. The shock gave way to defiance.

"But why do you need us? How did you even know we were connected to them?" Jules asked, hands on her hips again, her voice growing fierce. As far as she could tell, the people around her were pirates, and if the Time Empress was right, it was pirates who took her aunt and killed her mother. She had no tolerance for them, if that was who they were.

Kadian gave them an understanding nod and sighed quietly. He bent over and waved at Sprocket. The little dog bounced over to him and stopped short at his feet, tipping its head back and gazing happily up at the Captain.

"Sprocket was created by our ship's Chief Inventor, Marina Whelan." He lifted one hand and indicated a woman standing not far from him. She was slender and short, with sandy blonde hair that hung down to her shoulders and was parted in the middle of the top of her head, framing her pretty face. She gave them a wave and a friendly smile. Henry and Finn waved back. Marina was dressed in a tank top and cargo pants, the pockets of which were filled here and there with various and sundry items. Her skin was tanned and she had a little smear of some kind of oil on her cheek. Finn's eyes grew wide as she stared at Marina in awe.

Kadian continued. "Marina sent him to the Time Palace to find out what the Empress and the Guild Keepers knew about the time pirates. Unfortunately, the only information they had was that they knew time was being stolen in great quantities from a great many places, and no one could catch the time pirates at it." Kadian took another step toward them, gazing at their eyes.

"Sprocket sent a message to us when you arrived, telling us who you were and that you had gone to the Time Palace. We waited until you returned to Ramblewood, and then brought you here to find out if you might know anything about the Commodore... if there's any new discovery about where he and the time pirates are." Kadian's expression was so genuine that Jules found herself believing him for a moment, before something snapped in the back of her mind. He might be telling them that he was after the time pirates, but by all accounts as far as she could tell, he was a pirate, and she was not about to trust him so easily and quickly.

Biting at her lower lip thoughtfully, she considered everything that she and Henry knew. He glanced over at her and saw that she was in deep thought, and he waited, mouth closed, holding on to Finn's hand.

Kadian also watched and waited. Jules ran several scenarios through her mind and then finally spoke.

"We'll help you on one condition. You take the three of us with you." She demanded flatly. She would accept no other option. Henry blinked in surprise.

Kadian's brow furrowed and he shook his head, turning from her slightly. "I don't think that's a good idea. That won't do. Not at all." He gave August a deep look, and August shook his head as well, glancing down at Jules and holding her in his stoic gaze for a long moment before looking back at the Captain once more.

"It's not up for discussion." Jules stated, her arms crossed sharply over her chest as she eyed the Captain. "If you want to know what we know and you want our help, we go."

He reached his hand up and stroked his beard and moustache thoughtfully, looking over at August once more as the corner of his mouth turned up in a sly smile. "Well, since you insist. There is just one problem, though…" he trailed off, leaving August and walking toward Jules again, his boots sounding a soft thud on the deck with each step.

He drew near to her and searched her face. "We aren't quite sure where the time pirates might have taken Vianne. I wonder… perhaps you might know something about that. Perhaps it's possible that you heard something at the Time Palace while you were there, and you could give us some direction. After all, it's difficult to launch a rescue mission when we don't know where we're going. Tell me, lass, what you heard at the Time Palace, and we'll see if we can figure out where we're going to save your aunt."

Jules felt her stomach do a flip flop, and she wasn't at all certain that she could trust the man standing in front of her. "We didn't hear much about the direction she was taken in. We found out about other things." She replied vaguely, trying not to tip her hand so far that they'd get kicked off of the rescue mission. She didn't know where the pirates had taken her aunt, but she did know that sitting in the house at Ramblewood and doing nothing wasn't going to get Vianne found and saved, if she could be saved. The only real shot that she and Henry had at getting their aunt back was to stick to the crew before them and the ship they were on, and do all they could to learn the truth and go after Vianne.

Kadian frowned darkly. "You want to come along and you have nothing to offer in the way of information?" He sounded dubious.

She raised her brows at him, looking him straight in the eye. "I'm not telling you everything we know right here and now. I don't trust you. You're going to have to earn that. We're going with you, and that's all there is to it."

He tried to hide a chuckle at the corner of his mouth, and he turned away from her with his left hand resting once again on the elegant hilt of his sword. "You're a spitfire, you are. Fine then, you come, but you three must earn your keep. You will work around the ship learning different trades and helping out, and you must see to lessons with the ship's scholars and workers." He turned sharply on the children then, eyeing each of them seriously. "Do you agree?"

"I agree." Jules declared.

"As do I." Henry followed suit.

"And me." Finn added.

Captain Aragon nodded firmly. "Then we have an accord. You have already seen the cabin where you'll be staying. We will have an evening meal in the Wardroom tonight, and in the morning before first light, we will sail out of the cave and embark upon our journey."

Jules took a step toward him, uncertainty and excitement coursing through every part of her. "How can we start our journey if we don't know where we're going? Where will we begin?"

Kadian's eyes narrowed and she saw a smile beneath his moustache again. "Clever girl." He said with a quiet voice. "We will sail to the Port of Morrow, and with any luck, we can find some answers there. It's known to me as one of the stops for the time pirates, and it's a place to start. Now then, be off with you. Dress for dinner, and be in the Wardroom in twenty minutes." He walked away from them with August at his side.

A woman came forward from the crowd which had begun to slowly disperse, and she grinned at them, holding out her hand. She was darker skinned with black hair that was pulled back into a ponytail. She was curvaceous and full bodied, having a Puerto Rican look about her. "Hi, I'm Tamsin Cuevas. I'm the Electrotech Officer."

"Hello, I'm Henry, and this is my sister Jules, and our friend Finn." Henry replied, reaching out his hand to the lady.

She shook it, and then shook the girl's hands as well. "I know this is probably all a shock to you. If you like, I'd be glad to give you a helping hand to get you started."

"We'd be grateful for that." Jules answered with some relief.

Tamsin walked with them back to their cabin as Sprocket padded along beside them. When they reached it, she went in with them and entered their closet. "It's Captain's rules that anyone who joins him for a meal in the Wardroom, that's the dining room, is always dressed well."

She flipped through the hangers and pulled out a dress for each of the girls and a pair of khaki pants and a button up shirt for Henry that looked almost like what he was already wearing, though without the wrinkles. Henry took his clothes into the bathroom and changed while the girls dressed in the cabin.

When they were all ready, Henry ran his hand over the pants he was wearing and looked up at Tamsin. "It's curious that we were brought here and put into this cabin, and that clothes that suit our style and are made in our precise sizes are already hanging in the closet. It seems to me that the crew and Captain aboard this ship were already planning on us being here and staying." He eyed Tamsin, looking for an answer.

She gave him a wink and smile and shrugged her shoulder as she turned for the door. "That certainly is curious. Why don't I take you to the Wardroom." She led the way and said nothing more about the point that Henry had brought up.

Finn quickened her step and looked up at Tamsin as they walked. "What does an 'lectotech… uh…'" she trailed off as she tried to remember the job title that she had heard.

Tamsin smiled at her. "Electrotech Officer." She supplied the words that Finn couldn't find. "I'm an electrotechnician. I see to the electronic gadgets and gizmos on the ship, sometimes it's machinery, sometimes computers, sometimes other things altogether. All the electrics here work because I make sure they work." She gave them another wink, and they turned down a passageway and went through a set of light wood double doors.

The Wardroom was grandly appointed, with chandeliers of brass and crystal hanging at intermittent points along the length of the dining table that could easily seat thirty people; fifteen on each side, plus the Captain at the head and any guest of honor at the foot. The table was made of highly glossed mahogany, and around it every chair matched, and was fitted with a thick red velvet cushion. The dishes were all fine china, and the goblets were crystal. There were fresh tropical flowers in crystal vases along the length of the table, as well as eight count candelabras set every four feet along the center of the table.

The children's mouths fell open at the sight of it all. "Well I'll be knocked for six…" Finn gasped as she stared. "I never saw anything so pretty." She shook her head and pinched her own arm to be sure that she wasn't dreaming.

Tamsin placed a gentle hand at the girl's back. "This is beautiful, but wait until you see the rest of the ship. It's just as lovely in every place."

"If our cabin and this dining hall are any indication, I don't doubt it." Henry said quietly with a twist of his head.

Tamsin helped them find their finely written place cards sitting beside their plates, and she told them to stand behind their chairs and wait for the Captain. They were seated partway down the table to his left.

The officers of the ship began to enter the room, all of them finding their places and standing at attention behind their seats, until at last Captain Kadian, dressed in a tailored and stately coat, silk shirt, and pants, came in from a separate entrance, and he greeted them. When he pulled out his own plush seat and sat down, all the rest of the company followed suit, and so began the first and finest meal that any of the children had ever had.

The conversation was good among all of them, and the crew who were seated around the children made certain that all three of them were involved in it, not leaving them out of any part of it.

They met the Communications Officer, Anneliese Prichard, whose brown hair was combed back from her lovely pale face and tied into a practical bun. She was smart and short-spoken, though friendly and kind. Her form was thin, and even sitting, they could see that she was tall. She had a wide smile and red lips, which stood out from her fair complexion, along with her dark eyes and dark eyebrows.

They also met Paisley Parker, the Science Officer, who was wearing a deep purple jacket and pants with a lavender blouse. It complemented her dark skin and the short, black, curly hair that crowned her head. She was very pretty, with big brown eyes and full mouth. When she smiled at the children, they could feel her sincerity, and it was very easy to smile back at her.

Henry was seated beside Nicodemus Hawking, who seemed very old in many ways. His hair was white, his skin was light, and there were soft wrinkles all about his face and neck, though his hands looked strong. He was dressed in a dark brown suit with a white button up shirt and a little red bow tie. Nicodemus was the Ship's Astronomer, and when Henry learned that, he spent a good portion of the meal asking Nicodemus several questions. The children learned that Nicodemus worked in the ship's Observatory, and they were told that they could see it the next day when they went on a proper tour of the ship. All of them were excited for it.

When the meal was over, they all bid each other a good evening, and Jules waved at Captain Aragon, who had been watching them during much of the evening. He waved back at her in return.

Tamsin walked them back to their cabin and told them to be up, showered, and dressed very early, ready for the next day. Breakfast would be served in the Wardroom as well, and the children should dress for it, but as soon as the meal was finished, they were to put on casual clothes, and then would start their tour of the ship, and work for the day.

They thanked her and bid her a good night, and she beamed at them and left them to themselves. Sprocket, still in the shape of a dog, curled up on the floor and rested as the children sat on the sofa and chair in their pajamas, talking about all that had happened.

"I can't believe we're here." Jules said, shaking her head and running a brush through her long dark hair. "How on earth did this ever happen? This has been the strangest day ever!"

"Well, it's going to get a little stranger…" Henry trailed off, his eyes intent on the girls as he reached his fingers into the pocket of his nightshirt. "We have a stowaway."

"A stowaway? What are you talking about?" Jules asked, and Finn scooted to the edge of the sofa, her eyes on Henry's pocket.

With the greatest of care, he gently pulled his hand from the pocket, and resting in his palm was a strange looking worm. Its body was multicolored, and along its back and on top of its head was a trail of colorful and silky soft fringe. Finn gasped out loud and covered her mouth with her hand when she saw that the worm had an old looking face. She looked up at Henry and whispered, "I know him!"

Henry drew in a deep breath. "This is Rastaban. He's the librarian at the Universal Library in the Time Palace. He isn't normally this small, his real size is so big that he takes up a huge amount of space in the library, but he decided that he wanted to come along with us, and he shrunk himself down to this travel size so that he could fit in my pocket, and anywhere else that he needed to fit."

He held his hand out and Jules and Finn both came closer and stared, unblinking.

"Rastaban, you met Finn already, and this is my sister, Jules." Henry looked over at her. Rastaban gave her a slow nod of his head and spoke.

"What a wonderful honor it is to meet you, both of you." He turned to Finn and gave her a kindly smile.

Jules' mouth fell open. "He… he talks?" She whispered, trying desperately to wrap her mind around the concept.

"He does. He's really wise, actually. He's absolutely fascinating, to be honest." Henry began to grin as he looked down at the worm in his hand. "Quite remarkable."

"I've come along because Henry asked me to explain what I know about the Starlings, that is, your family. Also, I want the opportunity to get to know you better, and I need some adventure in my life. Real adventure. It's one thing to read about it in all of the books, but I suspect that it's quite another thing entirely to go out and live it." Rastaban told them; his voice still deep and resonating, even though he wasn't much bigger than Henry's finger.

"He's incredible!" Jules exclaimed, smiling wide at the little creature.

"I like him much better this size." Finn held her fingertips to her mouth as she let out a slight giggle, her eyes shining with delight.

"I do ask one favor of you," Rastaban told them seriously, "please do not let anyone know that I am here at all. I wish to keep my presence unknown, so that I may watch and listen as much as I can before anyone finds out about me. You see, the more we watch and listen, the more we know."

The children all agreed to the bookworm's request.

"Well, I'm not sure that I trust the Captain anyway." Jules lowered her voice. "I haven't made up my mind about him at all. It feels to me that he's got a lot of secrets that he isn't telling anyone."

Finn bit at her lower lip thoughtfully for a moment. "I could go and spy on him. I'm the littlest here, and I'm right good at sneaking around. I've had to be, in my old life. Want me to go and have a listen?"

Jules shook her head. "No, we all stay together. That's a rule I'm making and we must stick to it. We stay together." She gave the young girl a smile then. "I do like the idea of spying on him, though. Let's all go and we'll see what we can find out."

Henry and Finn agreed, and Henry put Rastaban back into his pajama shirt pocket. They slipped out into the corridor from their cabin, and made their way to an upper deck, and Finn told them that the Captain's cabin would likely be either on or near the deck.

Keeping to the walls and corners, they made their way silently around the rear deck until they found his cabin. Finn point out that one of his windows was open to the deck to let in the tropical night air.

The three of them huddled beneath the window, eyes on each other as they listened soundlessly. They heard two men's voices in the room; one was the Captain's, and it didn't take them long to decipher the owner of the other voice; it was August Holt, the first mate.

"What was all that bartering you did with the kids earlier? What kind of game was that?" August sounded frustrated. "You know they don't know anything more from the Time Palace than we do, yet you went along with that game, toying with them so they'd want to come along."

"I wanted them on the ship, and I knew the best way to do that was to make them think they'd demanded it and gotten their way. It had to be done. They have to be here." Kadian answered evenly.

"I don't like what's going on." August spoke in a low and troubled tone. "You know better than anyone just how ruthless the Commodore can be. It's not a good idea to bring those kids along. It's not safe. We should leave them where we picked them up, at Ramblewood. We don't need them. We should go on without them. Think of it. Nothing would happen to them there, only this crew knows about that place. Take them back."

"You're right, I do know just how dangerous it will be, and I wouldn't take them with us, but I have no other choice." The Captain sighed heavily.

"What do you mean? Of course you have a choice. You're the Captain! Take them back to Ramblewood and we'll be on our way!"

"Did you notice that chain around the older girl's neck? Jules Starling is in possession of a Cerellus. It's a time sphere. Only the Time Guardians get those, and each of those time spheres is coded by nature to the Guardian's bloodline. Because of their Starling heritage, they're the only ones who can use that time sphere!"

They could hear the thump of the Captain's boots as he paced back and forth in his cabin. "What's more, almost no one knows that those kids exist! By nothing short of a miracle, Marleigh and Vianne managed to hide those kids from just about everyone! Now, if anyone out in the universe discovers that those kids *do* exist, the both of them will be in grave danger!"

Henry and Jules stared at each other with wide eyes. The Captain sat down heavily in a chair that scraped over the floor a bit.

"I don't want to force them to use the Cerellus. I know it would be much better and undoubtedly easier if I made friends with them and then asked them to use it so that it could get me through time if I have to, in order to find and stop the Commodore. I can't leave something as valuable as those kids with that Cerellus sitting alone at a house. If we're ever going to get to the Commodore and get Vianne, we may very well need them!"

The children leaned in a little closer, but a sound nearby startled them, and they looked up to see the Ship's Inventor, Marina Whelan, standing a few feet away.

Their hearts pounded and they held their breath looking at her, knowing that they were caught.

Holding her finger to her lips, Marina pushed her straight sandy blonde hair behind her ear and listened for a moment, and then waved at them to follow her silently. They followed her.

Several feet down the deck, they rounded a corner and she stopped them beside a panel in the wall. Reaching her hand up to the side of it, she showed them an outline in the side of it, and she pressed her finger against it.

The panel slid inward and opened, revealing a passageway. "Stay to the left, and it will lead you to a door that reads 'passenger cabins'. That's the hallway where your cabin is."

She winked at them and helped them through the doorway. They whispered their thanks and she pressed the button again, and the panel closed. Soft, warm light filled the secret passage where the children found themselves. They walked quickly and quietly along it, staying to the left and going past other hallways that led off in other directions. Finally they saw a door that read 'passenger cabins'.

Henry and Jules looked around the door, and Finn spied a small outline on the wall. They pressed it, and the panel slid open, and they stepped into the hallway where their cabin was.

With a sigh of relief, they slipped into their cabin and closed the door behind them. Finn's sank down onto the sofa. "It's lucky that Marina was out late on the rear deck tonight!"

Henry looked at Jules seriously. "I think we should leave. We should go right away. This is no place for us. That August Holt obviously wants us back at Ramblewood. I think he's right."

Jules shook her head and reached for his hand. "Now wait a minute. Think about this. I know Kadian wants to use us, but even he said that no one can use this Cerellus except us. That means we have the upper hand." She pulled the pendant out of her shirt where it had been safely tucked away, and held it out by the chain in front of her. The sphere turned and swayed almost like a pendulum.

"I want to go." Jules stated firmly. "I want to find Vianne."

Finn reached for her hand. "I want to go, too. You are my new friends, and I haven't even met your Aunt Vianne yet. I want us all together back at Ramblewood."

Henry sank down onto the armchair and dropped his face into his hands. After a long moment he raised his head again and looked at Jules. "Okay. I guess we'll go, but we must remain vigilante. On guard at all times. I don't trust any of these people. There are secrets all over this ship. We stick together and we only trust each other." He insisted, standing back up again, his eyes on the girls.

"Agreed." Jules replied, giving her hand to her brother.

"Agreed." Finn added, placing her hand with theirs.

"Then it's off to the Port of Morrow before sunrise." Jules sighed, looking at the other two. "Wherever that may be."

Chapter Six

~
New Horizons

Sprocket woke the children in the predawn hours, and they slid from their beds sleepily at first. Finn laughed and pointed at the mechanimal.

"You're an owl! Why are you an owl?" She asked, going to him and touching his metal wings as he unfolded them.

"You'll be learning a lot today. You'll become wise. So I'm an owl today." He smiled at them with his beak and nudged Finn with it.

Jules looked around at them. "Well, Tamsin said that we should dress for breakfast, so let's get cleaned up and dressed, and then we'll go to the Wardroom."

A short while later they were all ready to go, even if they were still yawning. Sprocket took them to the Wardroom, and when they entered, the scents of a wide variety of foods entreated their noses to lead them to their seats. They waited until Captain Aragon sat, and then two men appeared to serve breakfast, as they had the night before when they had served dinner.

One of the men was tall and slender with broad shoulders. He had narrow eyes, thin lips, and a bald head. He was dressed formally, in a suit. He had introduced himself the night before as the Ship's Steward, James Dahl. He served the Captain and the half of the table nearest the head. The other half of the table was served by a man called Jonathon Strand, who was the cook. He was thin as well, with a withered face, a wrinkled old smile, and two bright blue eyes almost hidden by thick, bushy grey and white eyebrows. His hair, much the same as his eyebrows in color, was short and cropped around his head, making his ears look a little larger. He had a big nose, and it gave him a friendly sort of look, as a nice old man might have.

Seated with the children for breakfast were some of the faces that they had seen, belonging to people whom they had not yet met.

Henry was seated beside a man in a collarless, white button up shirt, with khaki pants like his. The man was young and strong, with sandy brown hair in small curls around his head, green eyes, a squared jaw, and a moustache.

He turned to Henry and held out his hand. Henry shook it and the man gave him a smile. "I'm Oliver Corliss. You're Henry Starling, right?" He asked, looking as though he not only knew that, but a great deal more as well. There was a twinkle in his eyes and the mark of mirth at the corner of his smile, just hidden beneath his moustache.

"Hello Mr. Corliss." Henry said, smiling back. "I am Henry. What is it that you do on the ship?" he asked curiously, as a list of possible occupations that the man might do flashed through his mind.

"I'm the Chief Aeronautical Engineer." Oliver answered. "You can call me Corliss. Everyone does."

Henry's eyes widened. "The Aeronautical Engineer?" He gasped. "Does this ship fly? Do you pilot the ship?"

Corliss laughed deeply and nodded his head. "The Gypsy Windlass does fly, much further than the blue skies above. You'll see that today, when we take off." He took a sip of his coffee and set the cup down. "The Captain and I both fly it, and we have a small team of aeronauts who all assist in the work it takes to get this ship through water, air, and the other places it goes." He gave Henry a wink, and Henry felt a thrill of excitement zoom through him as he wondered where else they would be going.

He and Corliss talked on, and Henry saw that the engineer was sharp, never missing anything that was happening around him, paying attention to every person and every action, his mind piecing it all together like a puzzle at light speed.

Henry already admired a few of the people he'd met onboard the ship, and Oliver Corliss was definitely one of them.

Sitting beside Jules was a woman with bronze colored skin and wavy dark hair that was tied in a ponytail at the side of her neck. She had big dark brown eyes that were framed with thick black lashes. She was trim and fit, smart and outspoken, and Jules liked her.

"I'm Trinity Barzetti." She introduced herself to Jules. "I'm the Ship's Culturalist. I'm so pleased to meet you."

Jules lowered a brow in confusion. "I'm really happy to meet you, too. What's a culturalist?"

Trinity gave her a warm smile. "This ship goes to many different kinds of places, and I'm something of an expert in the field of linguistics, customs, faiths and beliefs, histories, civilizations, politics, and geography. I learn really quickly, so no matter where we're going, I am a key resource to the Captain and the crew in making sure that we have successful interactions with any culture we encounter."

Jules blinked in surprise. "You do all that?"

Trinity winked at her. "I try my best to!"

They talked all through breakfast, and when it was cleared away, Trinity addressed the rest of the crew. "I'm going to take our young guests to the bow for the take-off, and then give them a tour of the ship. Does anyone else want to come along?"

Corliss grinned at Henry. "I'm in!"

Paisley the scientist, Nicodemus the astronomer, and Marina the inventor joined them, and little Sprocket, who was still shaped as an owl, flew along with them.

The group went to the front of the ship where the Bosun, Harley Silverstein; a short, round, hairy fellow with a thick cigar clenched in his teeth, got to work securing them for takeoff. He put a belt on each of them, and then clipped pencil thin steel cables which were drawn from the deck, to each of the belts. They could move about, but only in the area of the bow of the deck. Each of them were essentially leashed to the ship's surface.

Captain Aragon's voice could be heard on the loudspeakers all over the vessel. "Activate Shimmer! Commencing takeoff!" he announced officially. Everyone took their places, and a moment later, the anchor which had held them in the lagoon inside the cave, was lifted. Jules, Henry, and Finn held fast to the solid railing at the front of the ship, their eyes wide as the craft loomed forward toward the mouth of the cave and the falls. The crew in their company stood behind them, almost forming a human chain, to ensure the safety of the children.

Corliss called out to them over the roar of the water crashing down before them. "Take a deep breath! We're all going to get wet!"

Just then, the ship passed through the veil of cascading water, and everyone who was out on the open deck was drenched in fresh, cool water. The children all shrieked with joy and excitement, shivering with the shock of the cool water, but all three of them stayed fast where they were. They blinked rapidly and gasped, sputtering and laughing, sharing looks between themselves and looking over their shoulders at their new mates. The crew who stood with them were also soaked, and laughing just as much as they were.

Before the Gypsy Windlass lay the wide open sea, aquamarine around them, and cobalt blue in the distance. There were monoliths rising like titans out of the waves around them, dotted about with tropical trees, bushes, and seagulls. Behind them was a great island, edged with white sandy beaches and covered in lush vegetation. It looked like paradise, basking in the sun as a gem on the surface of the sea.

Jules felt like crying out, she was so filled with the thrill of adventure and the endless possibility before them, but when she did cry out, it wasn't because of her excitement. She, as well as Henry and Finn, cried out because thick billows of steam began to pour from the sides of the ship at even intervals, and a hissing sound came from the balloon behind them.

Sails swelled at both the fore and aft of the vessel, and they hadn't gone far at all when the ship lifted up out of the ocean and the sound of the water pouring off of the ship rivaled that of the waterfall they had sailed through.

The children gaped, peering over the bow, staring incredulously as the island and monoliths grew smaller beneath them, and the ship ascended swiftly into the heavens. The bright blue sky began to darken, and the parts of the land and sea beneath them that had been discernible, began to blur into each other, until the land was gone and all that could be seen was ocean.

Soon the clouds were around them, and then gradually as the ship continued heavenward, the clouds were below them. All around the ship, daylight faded and the blackness of space enveloped them. Stars and planets began to shine as if it was night, and the children's heads whipped from one side to the other as they looked about themselves, amazed at what they were seeing.

The Gypsy Windlass

Henry turned to the group of adults standing behind him. "Corliss! Sir!" He panted, every inner part of himself churning with anxiety. "What's happening? Where are we going? How is this possible? How are we still breathing and not freezing to death, or suffocating?"

Corliss smiled kindly and he, Nicodemus, and Marina stepped toward the three dumbfounded children.

"Activate Circadian Lighting!" August Holt called out over the loudspeakers. Gradually, the light all around the ship changed, and it was as if the morning sun was shining on them; it even felt warmer in the light, and there were shadows along the deck that might have been there if they had been in sunlight on the Earth.

"How did the light come back?" Asked Finn, eyeing the adults around them suspiciously.

"The natural light that you see and feel is called Circadian Lighting." Marina answered, tucking her sandy blonde hair behind one ear and then slipping her hands into her cargo pants pockets. "It's one of my better inventions, but I couldn't have done it without our scientist, Paisley. We travel through space a lot, and it's important for the health of the crew that we maintain our body's natural needs for regular daylight and nighttime hours. So, Paisley and I invented Circadian Lighting. We have fourteen hours of daylight and ten hours of darkness, every twenty four hours, all over the ship, no matter where we are on the ship. The daylight simulates a real day, so the light we see goes through phases like sunrise, morning, midday, afternoon, and sunset, before it gets dark. It's all gradual and natural feeling. It looks like morning right now, because that's the time that we left. It's much healthier for us, and keeps us on normal hours."

Henry shook his head and whistled low. "You're geniuses." He said in a voice filled with awe.

She smiled and shrugged. "We're in pretty amazing company. Several of us worked together to come up with many of the systems on the ship that make it do what we need it to do. You heard the Captain call for the Shimmer to be activated, well that was no small feat to create."

"What's a Shimmer?" Finn asked, looking back and forth between all of them.

Corliss held his hands up and used them to explain. "It's a kind of cloaking device. We don't want anyone on Earth to see the ship leaving the ocean or the atmosphere, and we don't want to be detected by radar or satellite, so a team of us, Paisley our scientist, Nicodemus our astronomer, Samuel who is our meteorologist whom you haven't met yet, Marina our inventor, and Shakti Sanna who is our machinist, and I don't believe you've met him yet either, all teamed up together with myself, to create a cloaking device that we call a Shimmer, to make us undetectable to sight or machines on Earth and in space. We had to take into account weather, atmosphere, debris that may move into the field around the ship, magnetic interference, and a host of other things, and we couldn't have done it if all of us hadn't worked together."

Jules began to beam. "Really? You all did that? No one can see the ship?"

Paisley nodded, crossing her arms over her chest proudly. "We did it. We called it a Shimmer because there's a single shimmering wave of light that moves once over the ship when we turn it on. It took a while to create and it was a great deal of work, but we did it. We've done a lot of things around the ship. Let's give you a tour, and you can see some of them. This is a very special craft, and it's probably best that you three know your way around if you're going to be living onboard for a bit."

With that, Trinity, Corliss, Nicodemus, Paisley, and Marina led the children away from the bow. Jules leaned over and whispered to Henry as they walked with their new mates.

"Is Rastaban with you?" she asked, giving him a surreptitious glance.

Henry nodded and patted the top of his shirt pocket with great care. Finn and Jules grinned and continued on their way.

"We should start with the Engine Room!" Corliss declared, excited to show the children where he worked part of the time, and what made the whole thing go. The others chuckled and nodded, walking together down the steps and through several passageways into the hull of the ship.

It was as if there was morning light all around them, and it felt to the children that if they were to look out of one of the windows, that they might see the ocean just outside.

Corliss stopped before a set of intricately carved wooden double doors, and beamed as he opened them, presenting the Engine Room.

The children only took four or five steps into the space before they stopped in their tracks and stared around them.

"I seen an engine room on the Swan, crossing over from Cork to America. This ain't an engine room, at least not the like of which I know." Finn reached her hand up and scratched at her nose as she took it all in.

Hanging over them were four brass and crystal chandeliers, glowing with soft light, in addition to the daylight quality glow in the room.

Henry's mouth fell open. "Chandeliers in the Engine Room?" He nearly whispered in astonishment.

"It's a fine ship indeed. Nothing left to mediocrity." Corliss said, resting his hands lightly on his hips as he gazed around the large room. It was two stories tall and though spacious, all of the area was used for one purpose or another. There were gauges and machines in many places, measuring tools, knobs, gadgets, gears, cables, and wheels. Throughout much of the room there was filigree metalwork ornamenting corners and poles, railings, and frames. Even the supporting beams that spanned from floor to ceiling were made of polished brass with elegant etched designs worked into them. The whole space had a truly Victorian look about it.

A brass spiral staircase led up to a brass walkway that spanned the perimeter of the room, where monitors and windows lined the walls intermittently. The children could see that they were in the middle of the ship, in the belly of it, though not at the bottom of it; there was still more space beneath the Engine Room on lower floors.

"This is spectacular!" Jules grinned in delight as she began to walk and look around at all of it. There were a team of men and women, about ten in total, who were working at different machines in various places in the room. A woman who was dressed similarly to Corliss approached them. Corliss clapped his hand on her shoulder.

"This is Mel. She's the Second Engineer on board the ship. I handle all the mechanics around the ship, and she maintains and operates much of what happens here in the Engine Room. She's also in charge of the Engine Ratings, which are the crew of workers you see here. She does an excellent job." He gave her a nod and she shook the children's hands.

Mel waved at a man who was at the far end of the room, and he came to them. He was tall and sturdy, bigger than any other man they had seen on the ship. He had no hair on his head, and his skin was the color of darkest chocolate. He had a kind and warming smile that made the children like him right away. He was wearing overalls and a loose shirt beneath them.

Corliss shook his hand when he reached them. "Jules, Henry, Finn, this is Shakti Sanna. He's our Ship's Machinist. He does a lot of our welding and building, as well as repairs. I'm certain that there's nothing he can't fix."

Shakti laughed deep in his chest, hearty and joyous. "Let's hope that always stays true!" He replied with a slight accent that none of the children could place.

Corliss raised one brow as he looked at the children. "Would you like to see the jewel of the ship?"

They nodded excitedly, and he took them and the rest of their company to the center of the Engine Room. Tamsin Cuevas was there, and she greeted the children with a happy wave and a smile. Finn waved and leaned forward, speaking quietly. "I remember you from when we were first on board. What are you doing here?" She asked inquisitively.

Tamsin looked over at Mel. "Well, Mel and I were monitoring the liftoff from Earth, as we used the balloon and sails for the Earth's atmosphere, but now that we're in space, we're switching the power for the ship over to the engine. You'll probably remember that I'm the Electrotech Officer, so I spend a good deal of time in the Engine Room when we're flying in space, making sure that everything is running as it should in here. She turned, and showed them what was behind her.

Four feet off of the floor on a steel platform, stood a rectangular crystal case, five feet long and three feet wide. At each of the corners was a brass column that held the crystal walls and the top of the case. Inside the casing was a reactor, taking up nearly all of the area inside the crystal box.

Corliss lifted his hand to point out the reactor as he explained it to the children. "Using a phenomenon called Cherenkov radiation, this reactor pulses, sending light through layers of crystal. Normally, nothing travels faster than the speed of light in a vacuum, which is what Einstein discovered, but there is a variation when light moves through what we call a refractive index, like water, ice, glass, or crystal. When light moves through those mediums, the protons are slowed down a little; the greater the refractive index, the slower the protons go, but the electrons continue to move at the same speed, and a strange thing happens."

Henry and Jules were staring at Corliss with rapt attention, but Finn's face was screwed up in confusion as she listened. "What happens?" Henry asked, almost breathless with anticipation.

Corliss smiled and continued. "Well, you know how there's a sonic boom when an airplane goes so fast that it breaks the sound barrier, and you can hear the boom really loudly for a great distance?"

Henry and Jules nodded and Finn frowned, totally lost.

"The same sort of thing happens with light waves. We have this engine case with layers of crystal inside it because crystal has a greater refractive index than water, ice, or glass. When the reactor pulses with a flash of light, the electrons going through the crystal move faster than the protons moving through it because the protons are inhibited by the crystal, but the electrons aren't, and it creates a luminal shockwave. Like a sonic boom, but with light. The shockwave powers the rest of the engine, and the rapid successions of luminal shockwaves that are produced propel us through space." He stood up and pushed his fingers down into his pants pockets, with a wide smile on his face; his eyes shining and his cheeks pink with pride. "A form of this technology is used on Earth, but the reactors there are kept in water to keep them cool. Because we only use this engine in space, there are ducts open from the outside of the ship to the engine, and even though the engine produces tremendous energy, it never even gets warm because it's nearly frozen by the coldness of space. This is exclusive technology. No one else even knows this engine exists."

"That is the coolest thing I've ever heard." Henry spoke with wide eyed reverence.

"That is pretty incredible." Jules agreed. Corliss was quite pleased.

"What's an airplane?" Finn asked with her arms folded across her chest. Corliss blinked in surprise at her.

"I'll tell you what, you and I will sit down at the computer, and I'll teach you about aviation, from the Wright brothers at Kitty Hawk in 1903 to present day on this ship. You can ask me all the questions you like as we go through it all." He gave her a kind smile and she returned a shy one to him as well.

Paisley chuckled, continuing where Corliss had left off. "Luminal shockwaves are one way that we power and move the ship. We also use the aether balloon and the sails, and there are actual nautical apparatuses onboard that enable movement through water when we aren't in the air or in space. One of the challenges that we encounter more often in space rather than on the Earth is magnetic fields or waves, and magnetism can severely compromise our instruments on the ship, particularly in the Engine Room, so you'll see that the entire ship, especially this room and everything in it, is made of steel, wood, brass, copper, glass, or crystal. None of those elements are affected by magnetism, so magnetic storms or interference by magnetism doesn't affect the way that the ship operates or any of its systems, including the Shimmer shield."

Mel perked up and waved at the children. "The Shimmer shield control is right over here." She walked over to a central control area, and showed them a steel handle that was pushed all the way up. "This handle operates the Shimmer shield. When it's all the way up like this, the shield is on and the ship can't be seen or detected. When the handle is pulled all the way down, the shield is off and everything is visible and detectable."

Finn cocked her head slightly and pointed to a large brass dial that had several different switches beside it, all flipped in the same direction, and next to each switch was a little green light. "What's that one for?" She asked interestedly. The whole Engine Room seemed to fascinate her, except for the physics of the engine, which she didn't understand.

Tamsin pointed to the dial. "That's the ship's gravity moderator. It controls the gravity and oxygen field around the ship; sort of like a bubble around the whole thing. The dial starts at zero, and when it's at zero, the ship has no gravity field; everything that isn't tied down could float off of it, if we are in space. After the zero, the dial moves in increments of ten degrees. So, one click over and we have ten degrees of gravity. Then twenty, then thirty, and so on, all the way up to ten, where it is now. With ten degrees of gravity, nothing is getting off of the ship without some propulsion, like a jet pack or jet boots. These switches to the right of it control gravity and oxygen in specific areas of the ship, like the library, the laboratory, or the garden, or any place on the ship where we want to leave gravity and oxygen on while other parts of the ship lose gravity and oxygen. We just flip the switches for the places where we want it all on, and then we can turn the gravity dial to zero. If the room light isn't green, there's no oxygen or gravity. It gives us more flexibility with the ship and control over what's going on."

Finn smiled. "That makes sense." She liked it, and it was easy to see that she liked understanding how the system worked.

Jules was captivated. "There's a garden on the ship?"

Henry brightened as well. "And a library and a laboratory?"

Marina laughed. "Okay Corliss, you've had your time with them here in the Engine Room. It's time to show them the rest of the ship. Let's head to the Science and Invention Lab." She winked at the children and everyone followed her, Trinity, and Paisley, as the three ladies led the way down a few more corridors and down a flight of stairs.

"We're in the dungeon." Marina teased with a light laugh.

"You'd never know it, though. It's really a beautiful space." Trinity added when she saw the concern on Finn's face.

They entered a single door, all of them walking in single file, and they found themselves in another large room. The lighting had gradually shifted to late morning, nearing midday, and the place they were in seemed bright and pleasantly warm.

Paisley spread her hand in an arc indicating the whole area. "This is where Marina, Trinity, and I work. This is the Science and Invention Laboratory."

There were big metal tables in different areas of the room, and though a few were empty, most of them were covered in beakers, Bunsen burners, tubes, trays, scraps of metal, glass, or wood, books, paperwork, charts, microscopes, jars, boxes, bottles, computers, notepads, and there were even a few scrolls laying on one table.

There were monitors and screens on three of the walls, and a big window and a thick glass door to an enclosed lab off to one side of the room, where Marina mentioned that they did experiments. Along two walls were counters with sinks, a wide array of measuring tools, and more machines of varying sizes and shapes.

The lab, though mostly made of and filled with metal and glass, still had the elegant look of carefully crafted design, like the Engine Room had, reminiscent of the style of the Victorian era.

Finn eyed Marina curiously. "Is this where you made Sprocket?" Sprocket flapped his owl wings and nodded happily. Marina patted him. "It sure is. He is one of my favorite creations."

Trinity pointed to a hallway that led out of the big room to another place. "That hall goes to the library. We use the library all of the time, so it made sense to have it close. I'm in the library more often than the lab." She began to walk toward the hall as she continued to speak. "The three of us frequently work with Nicodemus, our astronomer, and Samuel, our meteorologist." Marina looked over at Nicodemus who had been listening rather than speaking during most of the tour to that point.

Nicodemus reached his hand up and adjusted his glasses which were perched on the end of his nose. He pushed them up a little, closer to his eyes. "Our library has a wealth of information and it's useful to all of us, particularly when we are hashing out the science, math, and cultures of space life. There's much more that we don't know than there is that we do know, and working together as a team is nearly always the best way to accomplish an achievement in discovery or creation."

They all entered the library, which was the coziest room that they had been in by far. There were six desks set about in different places, all of them with stained glass Tiffany lamps and plush chairs. One of them had a computer on it that had been opened up from inside the desktop by lifting the desktop up and flipping it over, producing the computer. There was a steaming mug near the computer, and a pad of paper and a pen. The chair was empty.

The children looked around, especially Henry who was blissful that he had stepped into such a nice library. Some of the walls were straight, and some were curved to create nooks and quiet spaces. There were thickly cushioned seats and sofas around the room, as well as soft but good lighting, and Henry noted that there was fresh air coming in from somewhere. The room wasn't stale and musty as one might have suspected it to be.

Off in one corner, standing halfway up a ladder with three good sized books nestled into the crook of one arm, was a tall and thin man with dark brown skin and salt and pepper hair; naturally curly and cut close to his head. He had a pair of glasses on his nose and he had his head tilted back, gazing through the lenses of his glasses as he read the bindings on the books sitting on the shelf before him.

Nicodemus cleared his throat. The man turned his head slowly and looked at them and as he did, a smile crept over his face.

Moving down slowly from the ladder, he made his way to the desk and left the books he had been holding, then he walked toward the group.

"Well hello, I didn't realize that we had guests! I'm Samuel Calhoun. I'm the Ship's Meteorologist." He held his hand out to Jules.

"Hello, Sir. I'm Jules Starling, and this is my brother Henry, and our friend Finn." She shook his hand and gave him a friendly smile. She liked him. He looked as if he might be the kind of man a kid would want around as an uncle, if they were lucky.

"Please, call me Samuel. It's a pleasure to meet you. Are you joining us for long?" He asked, and Jules realized that she hadn't seen him up to that point, and there was a good chance that he didn't know anything about who they were or why they were onboard.

"We're probably going to be on the ship for a while. We're searching for our aunt, Vianne Starling. I guess we'll be around until we find her, but we don't know how long that will be." Jules explained.

Samuel frowned a little. "Well, if she's lost and we're out looking for her, I hope we find her soon." He said, speaking slowly and earnestly.

"We're giving our new mates a tour of the ship, and the Captain has ordered that these three help out with different jobs on the ship while they're aboard. Perhaps you could use some help with some of your work. I suspect they'd enjoy helping you now and then." Nicodemus told him with a twinkle in his old eyes.

"I would indeed. They could help us both, up in the Observatory or here in the library." Samuel replied. "What would you three think of that?"

"I'd love it." Henry answered right away.

The girls agreed right on the heels of his statement, and Samuel and Nicodemus grinned at them.

"We've got a lot more to see. Thank you, Samuel!" Trinity bubbled happily, giving him a wave as she led the group out of the library at the other end into another hallway.

Henry leaned down close to his shirt pocket and whispered to Rastaban. "It's a beautiful library, but it doesn't compare at all to yours." He heard the little bookworm laughing.

They went up a flight of stairs and down another passageway, coming to a single doorway.

Trinity knocked and then opened the door, and they all stepped into a spacious studio. There were thick mats on the light wooden floor, mirrors along two adjoining walls, and on the other walls there were rows upon rows of weapons for hand to hand combat, and a wide array of weights and workout accoutrement. In the center of the room, standing in a tense position with a gleaming steel katana in his hand, was a man in a loose fitting gi.

"This is the dojo." Trinity said, giving the man a wave. He eased his stance and lowered the blade, walking over to the group with a light in his eyes.

"Children, this is Katsuro Kuang. He is our Chief Combat Officer. Everyone on the ship is required to train with Katsuro regularly for hand to hand and weaponry combat. I think it would be wise if all three of you came here to train with him as well while you're staying on the ship."

Trinity looked at the Asian warrior then. "Katsuro, this is Jules and Henry Starling, and their friend Finn."

Jules was fascinated. "It's a pleasure to meet you, sir. What styles of martial arts do you teach?"

He gave them a lopsided grin, and they saw at once that he had a good sense of humor, though his eyes remained serious. "I teach many kinds. Aikido, Jujutsu, Judo, Karate, Kendo, Kung fu, T'ai chi, and Tai kwon do. I also teach western style fencing and some forms of wrestling. I request you come to dojo every morning before breakfast for training. There is much for you to learn. No better time to start learning than present. Will help you build up good appetite; you will eat much and grow healthy and strong." He grinned at them.

Finn and Jules nodded eagerly, but Henry looked a bit more reserved. Jules replied, "We'll be in first thing tomorrow morning."

"I will make certain we have gi for each of you to wear. You will train barefoot." Katsuro advised them. They thanked him, and Trinity led them back out into the hallway, forward on their tour.

"You all train in that dojo regularly?" Henry asked in surprise.

"All of us, regularly." Nicodemus answered him, and Henry looked up in amazement at the old man, realizing at that moment that the only person on the ship whom he had seen out of shape was the Bosun, Harley Silverstein. He considered that they were heading off looking for time pirates, and that it might well do them a great benefit to have some kind of defensive skills at hand.

Their tour wound through the ship to the Sick Bay where they met the First Medical Officer, Dr. Juric Van Pelt, who was sturdy and tall, with platinum blonde hair and bright blue eyes. He showed them around and the children were most impressed with the top notch medical facilities on the ship.

Finn mentioned quietly that her life might be very different had such fine facilities been available to them on the Swan when she crossed from Cork to America. She said that her parents might have survived the Cholera that killed them en route.

They saw the communications office, which was alight with computers and various other tools of communication. The only person in the room was Anneliese Prichard, whom they'd met at dinner their first night. Her dark brown hair was pulled back into a bun, and her thickly fringed brown eyes and red lipstick mouth still contrasted highly with her very fair toned skin. She had the same wide and bright smile for them, giving them a swift look around her office before she went straight back to work and they were led out.

Trinity expounded upon the communications officer's job. "She has several means of communication in there, so that no matter where we go on Earth or in space, she can effectively communicate with other ships, worlds, or cultures. She works with me whenever there is a cultural or linguistics question."

They next went to the ladders that were tethered to the deck and stretched up to the platform around the widest part of the balloon. The children held on tight as they all climbed up the ladder one by one, until they were on the mid-platform at the guard house.

It was there that they met the Flight Chief, Lukas Tendaji. He had a bronzed and exotic look about him, along with a warm and welcoming smile. He showed them around the guard house, introduced them to some of the many men and women working on, in, and around the balloon, and patrolled with them around the perimeter of the balloon. It was one of the most thrilling parts of their tour, to be up so high with not much to hold on to but the beautifully designed steel railing. Finn was inspired by all that she was seeing, and tremendously impressed by it.

"Mr. Tendaji, Sir?" She asked, meeting his dark eyes with hers. "How many people work on this ship?"

He gazed down at her and then sank to his knees so that he could look her in the eye at her level. "There are dozens and dozens. The people who work on the deck are called the Deck Ratings crew, then there is the Cabin crew, those who work in the Engine Room are the Engine Ratings, on the bridge and up here on the platform we have Helmsmen and Flight crew, there are workers in the Gunnery & there's the artillery crew, along with the Chief Gunner. There's a Science team and there are assistants to all the key leaders on the ship. There's a Ship's Clerk, the medical crew, and the kitchen crew who work for our Steward James Dahl, and the chef, Jonathon Strand, though you most likely won't see them unless you work in the kitchen at some point."

"My goodness! That's a lot of people!" Finn exclaimed in wonder. Henry and Jules were just as astonished as the young girl was.

"It is indeed." Tendaji agreed. "Let's show you the rest of the flight deck."

He led them up the ladder that ran from the guard house platform to the top center of the great balloon. There they stood on a circular platform and took in a tremendous view of space around them, before Tendaji pressed a button and the platform sank gradually down through an exquisitely designed brass and transparent glass shaft that ran straight through the center of the balloon and opened onto the main deck. Tendaji explained that the elevator platform gave them the best access to anywhere inside the balloon for maintenance.

The children were surprised to discover cables, iron catwalks, cords, and spiral staircases all throughout the interior of the balloon; they had expected it to be empty.

Tendaji showed them aether chambers within the balloon in the shape of wedges, which inflated and deflated according to their need for use. Henry was fascinated with it all.

When they left the shaft, Nicodemus and Samuel led the company to the Observatory on the quarterdeck of the ship.

Jules' eyes widened as she saw it. It was a standalone structure, practically its own building, with an extraordinarily unique design.

"It looks Arabian!" She wondered aloud as they approached it. It was fair sized, taking up a third of the quarterdeck and standing at two stories with a sculpted turret at the top of a tower on one corner. The turret reminded her of her aunt's house, where there was a similar turret design on the roof. There was a great metal dome over the rest of the Observatory.

"The design of the observatory was created with the Arabian's in mind as a sort of nod of respect to the work they contributed to astronomy throughout the ages." Nicodemus explained.

Jules frowned. "I didn't know that Arabian's contributed anything to astronomy. I've heard lots about Copernicus, Ptolemy, and Galileo and other astronomers, but none of them were Arabian."

Nicodemus gave his head a shake. "That's no surprise. You see, while most of Christendom was out fighting holy wars, many Persians or Arabs were studying the heavens. Consequently, most of the stars which were first discovered and charted have Arabian names. For example, from here we can see the Summer Triangle, which is Vega, Altair, and Deneb, just there." He pointed to a massive triangle formed by three bright stars, off to the side of the ship.

With a sorry sigh, he continued. "I don't believe it's common for mid-eastern astronomical history to be taught in the west; there is still a considerable conflict between the mid-east and the west. The Christians didn't even want to accept scientific advances in astronomy from their own brethren. The Catholic church put Galileo on trial and then under house arrest for the remainder of his life when he persisted with the teaching of his book *Dialogue* which supported the Copernican hypothesis of heliocentric theory. Basically, he said that the planets revolve around the sun, and he was condemned to life imprisonment for it in 1633. The church didn't retract that until 1992.

Nevertheless, the Arabians or Persians had a great deal to do with the discoveries that gave us the knowledge we have about our universe now. So, the observatory was designed with a nod of respect to those scholars who lived long ago and paved the way for us today."

Samuel opened the door of the observatory and they all stepped inside. Like the rest of the ship, the observatory was beautifully designed with Victorian elegance, though there were no chandeliers hanging from the ceiling. The ceiling was a transparent metal dome created by Marina, which opened and turned in a full circle to allow the crew to look through the enormous telescope that was housed within the center of the observatory. It was twenty-seven feet long with a twenty-nine inch lens.

There were several other scopes of varying sizes, which Shakti Sanna had fixed to the walls all around in such a way that they could easily glide out on an arm and be pointed in any direction for use. Though most of the room was outfitted with viewing instruments, gauges, compasses, tools, and astronomical machinery, there was one section of wall that was completely devoted to computers and monitors. At that place, and in a few other places, were desks and tables set with more computers and gadgetry.

Rastaban couldn't resist peeking out of Henry's shirt pocket to see it all; he was as intrigued by it as the children were.

Nicodemus handed each of the children a red laser pointer and showed them how to use it to point out far away things in the darkness. Each of them enjoyed it, though Finn had the most fun with it, starting the game of a laser beam sword fight with Jules.

After a look around the observatory and some time to work with the scopes and instruments, Trinity announced that it was nearly teatime.

"How much more of the ship is there to see?" Henry asked, knowing that they had hardly seen half of it.

Trinity raised her brows. "Actually, there's quite a bit remaining. There's the Operations Room, which we use in a battle for strategy and planning, the Bridge where Captain Aragon works with August Holt, the brig, the morgue, the meditation room, the Helmsman's house at the bow of the ship, the hull, the exploratory pod which we call the Pearl, and several other cabins on the cabins deck. You haven't seen the parlor either, but we're going there for tea now, so you can cross that off of your list, and I think after tea you should each choose a room to begin your work and studies in for the remainder of the day. You have plenty of time ahead to see the rest of the ship. It would be a lot to do it all today."

The others agreed, and the group went down to the middle deck at the rear of the ship, where they stepped into the parlor. It was a luxurious room, with thickly cushioned velvet seats, sofas, and a few armchairs. There were wide, slightly rounded windows framed by dark red velvet curtains, that looked out of the back of the ship, offering a stunning view of space behind them. There were tables made of highly polished wood and a large chandelier hanging from the center of the wood paneled ceiling.

Kadian and August joined them, and moments later, James the Steward entered the room pushing a brass cart filled with three tiered plates loaded with cakes, pastries, and sandwiches. Jon followed him pushing a matching cart holding a brass tree standing two feet tall, loaded with gently arched thin branches. At the ends of each branch hung a fine china teacup, while the teapot rested in a hollow within the trunk of the metal tree, where a copper warming base kept the teapot heated. It was another of Marina's inventions.

In no time at all, they were seated and served afternoon tea, and Jules, Henry, and Finn could scarcely believe that they were sitting in such a beautiful room on the back of a ship which was their new home, sailing through space and having tea with a team of some of the greatest minds the Earth had known.

Kadian looked at all three of them and raised his brows questioningly. "Have you met most of the crew and seen the ship?"

The children nodded. "Yes." Jules answered with a smile.

Henry gave his head a shake. "It's magnificent!"

Kadian nodded and smiled. "I'm pleased that you like it. We've taken the greatest care in building it and assembling the best possible crew for it. I'm glad that I have it, because we're going to need it to find and rescue Vianne.

Chapter Seven

~

Voyagers

When they had finished tea, everyone in their group went to work, and Kadian and August took the three young ones to the Bridge on the quarterdeck, beside the Observatory.

The forewall of the bridge was halved; from the wooden floor upward a yard, there was a burnished brass wall, and from the edge of the wall to the ceiling, there was one-sided unbreakable glass. Anyone on the inside could see out, but from the outside, like the dome atop the Observatory, anyone looking at it wouldn't see a window, it looked like a steel fortification.

At the place where the window began, was a slanted brass counter panel that spanned the full length of the wall and was nearly filled with gauges, dials, switches, buttons, and knobs. In the center, a large monitor was set into it so that it was flush with the surface. The monitor showed several different smaller screens, all providing different information simultaneously.

At the center of the room was a large old fashioned ship's wheel with a brass center, used to steer the ship.

Two walls of the bridge were lined in rolled up scrolls held fast by filigreed brass brackets at the sides. The third wall looked much like the front command counter; it was made of burnished brass and was filled with similar accoutrement and held two sizeable monitors, though only one of them was on.

Henry walked toward the back and far side walls which held the rolled scrolls. There were dozens of them; one directly above another, directly above another, all the way to the ceiling. "What are these?" He asked, captivated by them.

Kadian smiled. "Those are maps. Maps of lands, seas, uncharted territories at least to a point, planets, star systems, galaxies, constellations, black holes, and much more." He set his hands on his hips as he watched the boy. "Choose one."

A grin crept over Henry's mouth and he walked to one that was as high as his waist, stretching his hand out and touching the brass bracket at the side of it. He looked over his shoulder at Kadian. "This one."

Kadian walked to it and reached for the shining brass handled secured at the edge of the vintage looking scroll. He grasped the handle and gave it a pull, and the parchment unrolled to five feet in length. Kadian let go of the handle and the map stayed right where it was.

Finn's mouth fell open and she bent over a bit to look under the map to see what was holding it up, but there was nothing there. She stood back up and furrowed her brow in confusion.

Jules, Henry, and Finn gazed at the map which by all accounts looked to be an old parchment map, though after only a moment they realized that the lines, images, and shapes on it were moving slightly.

Henry blinked in surprise and looked up at Kadian, who was doing his best to hide a smile beneath his moustache. "It's… it's moving! Is it digital?" He asked, endeavoring to make sense of it.

Kadian gave a laugh. "You could say that, yes. Go ahead and touch it."

Jules and Henry both reached out a finger and pressed their fingertips to the surface of it, while Finn laid one of her small hands on it. She looked up in surprise at Kadian and August. "It's hard!" She gasped.

Kadian walked over to it and touched his finger to the fanciful compass drawn at the corner of the map. The map suddenly sprang outward off of the parchment, and formed a 3D map that filled the room, surrounding them. The men and children found themselves standing within the interactive, digital map.

"Wow!" Jules exclaimed, and Henry laughed as he turned in a circle where he stood, looking all over the room at the different parts of the map that had just been on the surface of the paper. Every element of the map was lit up. It so happened that Henry had chosen a map of Earth.

Kadian watched them with some amusement. "Touch any part of it." He said with a pleasant tone.

Jules reached her hand up just a little higher than her face, and touched Africa. The rest of the world disappeared, and all of Africa filled the room, or at least the shape of it did. It was colored like a cartoon; each country on the continent was a different color, and the sea around it was sky blue.

"Tell the map you want to see virtual imagery." Kadian told them.

Henry lifted his chin and spoke clearly. "Show virtual imagery." He repeated after the Captain. The cartoon coloring on the map disappeared, and a crystal clear landscape appeared over the continent, from the Sahara desert to the deepest jungles; it was all right in front of them, moving, and looking as real to them as if they could reach out and touch it.

"It even shows different weather patterns!" Henry marveled at what was all around him. "Look, it's raining in the jungle, and there's a dust storm in the desert." He tilted his head and looked up at the Captain. "Does this map show what's indicative of the weather in an area, or does it show what's really happening? Is it really raining in the jungle there right now?"

Kadian nodded. "It's real-time weather, and real-time; you see the light moving over the continent; that's the daylight that's happening as we speak." The children were amazed.

Finn walked through the glowing projection toward Egypt. "I heard of this place. This is where they have the pyramids, isn't it?" She said in a quiet voice. She reached out and gently touched her finger to the bluish river that flowed there. The river seemed to fill the room then, flowing all around them as if it was real, showing the riverbanks, people, cities, and wildlife there. A feminine voice spoke, and the children jumped a little, looking around as they tried for a moment to detect the source of it.

"The Nile River. The Nile is the longest river on Earth, at four thousand, one hundred, and sixty miles in length from its principle source, Lake Victoria, to its delta in the Mediterranean Sea. It flows in a northerly direction through three countries on the continent of Africa; Uganda, Sudan, and Egypt. It has remained a vital center of trade, culture, agriculture, transportation, and a life support system for the regions through which it flows since ancient times." The voice instructed.

"Wow!" The children echoed each other.

"Close." Kadian spoke in a clear tone.

The 3D map closed, and all the digital imagery around them vanished, leaving only the scroll with the moving lines and images on its surface. He walked over and touched the delicate handle at the edge of the map, where it was hovering above the floor, and the map rolled itself back up until it was set against the wall just as it had been when they walked onto the Bridge.

"That was amazing!" Henry cried out, his whole body humming with excitement. He heard Rastaban in his pocket as the little bookworm spoke.

"I really need to see about getting those for the library at the Time Palace!" he said quietly. Henry chuckled softly.

Kadian waved his hand at all of the maps. "These are but a few of the hundreds and hundreds of maps that we have, though what isn't on the walls here is stored in the computers. We can open them all up the way you've just seen, and explore what we like as we stand here. You can access all of them in the library, or indeed in any room on the ship, if you're inclined to study them. We make new maps every time we come to an uncharted area or place, and everything we make is stored and saved."

"They're so wonderful!" Finn was as thrilled as Henry was. "I can't wait to see more of them!"

"Then I'll indulge you and let you choose one more before we go on to other things." Kadian said kindly, giving the girl a smile.

Finn nodded and reached for a map on the other wall. "This one!" She cried out excitedly. Henry and Jules were a little surprised to see the girl react so openly; she had been mostly quiet and closed off since they had left Ramblewood. In both the Time palace and on the ship, she hadn't said much, and they had wondered if she was alright. Seeing her enthusiasm gave them contentment in knowing she was okay.

Kadian went to the map while August tended to the control panels for the ship, monitoring them and making slight adjustments here and there to various knobs, dials, and switches.

With just a few touches as before, they were suddenly surrounded by what was on the map, and the map was a section of space.

"Outer space!" Finn beamed, having learned the term the day before from Henry.

"I can see worlds, and stars, and galaxies!" Henry exclaimed, trying to take it all in at once.

Jules frowned a little and walked through the 3D map to a spot nearer the other side of the room. There were little balls of light moving, and she pointed to them, looking back over her shoulder at Kadian. "What are these? They're only appearing and vanishing in this one place!"

The Captain took a few strides across the room toward her. "That's a shooting star field. There are many of those. We're careful about flying around those rather than through them, because we have gravity on the ship and we don't want the shooting stars drawn to us; they would damage the ship. It is beautiful to pass by a field when they are falling on something else, though."

"What are these small blue dots? They sort of form a line… a pattern, almost, don't they!" Finn was studying one of the more unusual aspects of the map they were looking at.

"Those are spaceports, not unlike the one we are headed toward." Kadian answered.

Before he could say another word, Henry gasped, his hands reaching for the slanted panel at the front window on the forewall. "Captain! What is that? At the front of the ship! Look!"

They all looked. Breaking all around the bow of the ship were huge swells of light in different colors. Kadian smiled. "Those are light waves. The light waves are traveling through space, and we got lucky enough to travel across one of the waves." He reached over to a switch on the panel and flipped it, then spoke a little louder. "Bosun! Report to the Bridge!"

Not two minutes later, Harley Silverstein knocked on the door of the Bridge, and Kadian opened it wide to him. "Mr. Silverstein, if you would please, take our guests to the bow to show them the light waves."

Harley had a thick cigar sticking out of the corner of his mouth, and he yanked it out and held it in his fingers while the Captain spoke to him. "Yes, Sir!" He replied, giving the Captain a salute that left a trail of cigar smoke in its wake.

Kadian frowned at him. "Put the cigar out while the children are with you."

Harley nodded. "Of course, Sir!" He killed the glowing cherry at the end of it by lifting his foot off of the deck and stubbing his cigar out on the heel of his boot. Moments later, he was leading the children away from the bridge toward the bow.

The three of them stood abreast at the railing, holding fast to it as they watched ripple after ripple of light build before the ship, rising up over the bow like a splashing ocean wave, and then subsiding behind the ship.

"Mr. Silverstein, how is it that the light reacts this way with the ship?" Henry asked, fascinated by what they were watching.

Harley shrugged. "Waves is waves. No matter if they are waves of water, or sound, or light, or energy, or radiation, or even magnetic waves. They is all waves and they all act the same."

Henry nodded and turned to look back at them as Harley worked nearby. Rastaban had poked his rainbow fringed head out of Henry's pocket, and he was thoroughly enjoying the wonder of the light waves washing over them.

"This is magnificent!" He cried out blissfully. "I've read about them so many times in books, and I've never seen them. They're beautiful!"

When the light waves had dissipated and the ship was moving forward through darkness once more, James the Steward came to them, and told them that they had kitchen duty with him and John, preparing the evening meal.

Jules, Henry, and Finn followed him down to the kitchens, which they had not yet seen. The kitchen was designed with light wood floors and almost everything else looked to be either copper or brass. Half of the large room seemed to be a little more old fashioned, while the other half was a wonder of state of the art electronics, and somehow it all blended well together.

Jonathon Strand, the old cook, was leaning against the brass counter with his ankles crossed and his arms folded over his chest. His bright blue eyes shone out from under his bushy grey and white eyebrows. He gave them a wide smile and all the wrinkles on his face were pushed upward and outward.

"Welcome to the galley!" He called out to them, bringing his hands out to his sides in grand way, presenting the room to them. "Now let's get to work." He turned then and indicated three work stations lined up side by side. There was a step stool before the sink and beside the sink was a large bowl full of potatoes and carrots. In the sink was a colander. Beside that were two cutting boards with knives and at the end of the assembly line was a big pot.

Finn spied the set-up and pushed her sleeves up to the elbows. "Right. Well I know about washing and peeling potatoes, so that will be me on the stool." She went straight to it and got to work. Jules and Henry followed her, and in no time, they were blazing through not only potatoes and carrots, but a host of other vegetables as well, for the stew that Jonathon was creating.

As they worked, a bright light began to shine in through the windows, and the children leaned and looked, trying to see what it was.

"Where's all the light coming from?" Henry asked curiously, rising up on the tips of his toes and seeing nothing but the light.

James, who was preparing wine, looked over at Jonathon who was tenderizing meat. "They've got it done nearly twice over. Why don't we take them up on the deck for a quick break and have a look. What do you say?"

Jonathon walked over to the sinks and the pot and smiled approvingly. "You've all done quite well with your work. Let's go on then and have a look as our Steward suggests. I could use a little fresh air myself, but not more than five minutes. We've plenty more to do in here!" He set his meat tenderizer down and the five of them walked up the stairs to the deck.

Off the starboard bow was a great red star, shining brighter than any they had ever seen, though they had also never been so close to one before, save for the sun.

"It's red!" Finn exclaimed in surprise. "Why's it red?"

The children were lined up at the railing, leaning on it, and Jonathon and James each stood at the ends of the row of young ones, leaning on the railing themselves.

"It's a red supergiant." Jonathon told them. "That one will become a mine for Star Iron in the near future. The cores of many stars are converted to iron in the natural life cycle of a star. There are space miners who go out to mine the iron cores of stars, though not all of them mind you. If that red supergiant there was smaller, it would degenerate into a neutron star, and if it was bigger, it would collapse in upon itself until it disappeared completely and it would become a black hole."

All three children were mesmerized by what they were learning. James, not wanting to miss out on any of the excitement, added his own bit to the discussion. "All of the iron on this ship is made of Star Iron. It's quite a pretty penny to come by, but it's well worth it."

Jonathon stood up and waved his hand at them. "Alright. It's been five minutes. Let's get back, we've got a hungry crew to feed!" They all followed him back down to the kitchen and he put them straight back to work. They didn't complain, and each of them rather enjoyed having the culinary tasks to do for their new friends.

When the evening meal was served and cleared away and the children had helped with the dishes, the three of them went out onto the deck and found a quiet spot to watch everything that they were sailing past.

"I know we've been here a couple of days now, and maybe I should be used to it, but I'm just not. This is so surreal, that there are three of us, that we picked you up in New York in 1849, Finn, and that now we're all three working and living on a *ship*… a ship that's sailed away from our planet and is making its way through space to a space port! It's absolutely unbelievable!" Henry shook his head as the truth of it all sunk into his brain and he considered it fully. "I'd never have believed it possible, any of it, if someone had told me a week ago that I'd have a sister and be doing any of this. It's just impossible."

"I know what you mean. I wouldn't have believed it either. Look at us… is that a comet way off over there? I think that's a comet! How did we even get here? How is any of this real?" She shook her head. Then she turned toward Finn, who was watching space and looking back at them now and then.

"I think it must be easier for Henry and me, Finn. At least we aren't too far removed from our own realm of reality; I mean, in our time people have traveled in space and gone to the moon, and we have electronics. We can understand how many things on this ship work. You though… you're coming from a time where there wasn't even electricity or even indoor plumbing, really. This has all got to be so unreal and incredible to you, but I have to say, you're really handling it like a champ." Jules gave her an encouraging smile and nod.

Finn thought about it for a moment and then shrugged. "Well, I really like the electricity and the plumbing. Actually, it's all a million times better than where I was back in Ireland. I love Ireland, but we was all having such a hard time that we had to leave. We left hoping for a better life. That's what me Mum and Da wanted for me, and now, strange as it is, I'm in a better life. No matter how strange it might be, I'll take it. I'll work it out as I go. I had to work out how to live in New York on my own, livin in the streets, and I did. I worked hard to change the way that I speak so people wouldn't know right away that I was Irish; most people didn't like Irish folk. I tried to sound more like I was from England to fit in better. No one cares here. It's all strange and different, but it's better. Besides, it's really interesting."

She grew quiet then and pulled her skinny legs up to her chest, resting her chin on her knees. "I just miss my family, but they was already gone when I got to New York, so it's not like I left them behind when I came here. I had nothin and no one back there. Now I got you two, and I got a good place to sleep; best I ever had, and I got good food three times a day. And do you know I ain't seen one single rat on this ship? It's clean. It's strange, but I'll take it, even without my family."

Jules felt a lump form in her throat and her eyes stung. She couldn't stop the tears that formed in her eyes and spilled out onto her cheeks. "I miss my mom so much, and I wish we had Aunt Vianne with us, too."

When Henry saw her crying, he couldn't stop himself from crying either. "I miss Vianne as well. You're right Finn, we're in a good spot, but it's hard to be here without the people we love most."

Jules gave Henry a meaningful look, and then reached out for Finn's hand. "Finn, I promise you that when we find our Aunt Vianne, you can stay with us as long as you like, if you want to. You can be our younger sister, and then none of us will ever be alone again."

Rastaban poked his head up out of Henry's shirt. "I think that's a beautiful idea. It's truly wonderful."

Finn managed a half smile, and she reached her other hand out to Henry, so that she was holding hands with both Starlings.

There were soft footsteps behind them, but they didn't hear them in time to dry their eyes and cheeks. They looked up to see Nicodemus, who had come from the Observatory. He knelt down close beside them.

"Is everything okay?" he asked, looking at each of them in turn.

"We're just missing our families." Jules answered as lightly as she could.

He nodded understandingly. "I miss mine too, sometimes. Hey now, why don't you three come with me." He stood up and they got to their feet and followed him.

Nicodemus led them to the elevator platform inside the pillar at the center of the great balloon on deck. They rode it all the way up through the balloon to the crow's nest platform at the very top of it. There they held fast to the railing and looked out at the darkness around them.

"I come up here when I need to clear my head. It's peaceful and beautiful." He turned and looked at the children then, gazing at each of them in the eyes. "Your pasts are behind you, but your futures are as wide open as the space that stretches out before us. It's all possibility; you must remember that."

Finn tilted her head and gave him a curious look. "How big is outer space?" She asked, using the phrase again and liking it.

Nicodemus lifted his chin and looked out at it. "It's endless, with endless dimensions and endless worlds. We know much, but even that is a speck of nothing to what's out there."

She turned and looked out at the vastness of it as well. "When we was on the crossing from Ireland, I went out on the deck of the ship almost every night and watched the night sky. I wondered what was up there and how far it went. When we got to New York City, I couldn't see as much of it as I could out on the ocean, and I missed it."

"The stars and the heavens are always there, whether you can see them or not, just like the people who love us." Nicodemus reached his arms around all three children and held them closer.

Chapter Eight

~

Secrets

Jules tossed and turned that night, not able to sleep well at all. Her mind was a torrent of memories both real and imagined, of dreams that were fearful and terrifying.

At long last she gave up trying to sleep and she slid quietly out of her bunk and pulled her robe on, nestling her feet into her slippers. Giving the other two a watchful eye to make sure that they were sleeping well, she then checked on Rastaban, who was sleeping peacefully in his little garden box that Henry had made for him in the lab, and she peeked at Sprocket, who was in the form of a teddy bear and was sitting beside Finn as she slept.

Jules held her finger up to her lips and quietly shushed Sprocket. He gave her a slight nod, and she slipped out of the room and into the hallway, closing their cabin door softly behind her.

With the deft movements of a ninja, she stealthily made her way down the hall to the secret passageway, and she took that to the main deck. Once there, she returned to the quiet spot that she, Henry, and Finn had found earlier. Jules sank down onto the deck and brought her knees to her chin, resting her arms on them and burying her face.

Somehow she felt free to cry. She didn't have the responsibility and worry of being the big sister and of needing to look out for the younger two. She didn't feel that she needed to be 'on', wearing a poker face as she made her way around so many new people on the ship, pretending to be braver and stronger than she felt. She could, at least for that moment, be herself and let out all of the emotion and pain that she had bottled up inside of her.

She wept a long while, but not too long after her weeping had eased and diminished to soft breathing, she saw the light on the ship begin to change, as if the sun was about to rise over it. She remembered that the ship operated on false lighting to maintain normalcy, and she wiped at her eyes and cheeks, knowing that it would mean the rest of the crew would be up and working in no time, and the miniscule night crew would be heading to bed.

Suddenly, there was someone beside her, and she drew in a sharp breath, her eyes shooting upward to see who it was. She was surprised again to see that it was the Captain.

Kadian was dressed as he had been since they'd met him, wearing all black, his beard trimmed close to his squared jawline, and his leather boots much quieter than she had realized.

He knelt down beside her. "Are you alright?" He asked, his sky blue eyes held fast to hers with concern.

She sighed heavily. "I'm okay." She hesitated, but something about him made her feel that she could trust him. "I just couldn't sleep. I'm just missing my mom a lot." A new tear escaped her eyelashes and rolled down her cheek. She didn't move to brush it away, but the Captain wrapped one arm around her shoulders and hugged her. She leaned her head in to him and let another tear fall.

Kadian closed his eyes and nodded. "I know how you feel. I miss Vianne terribly."

Jules lifted her chin in an instant and stared at him. "What?" She asked, completely confused.

He bit at his lower lip thoughtfully for a moment and then sighed and stood up, holding out a hand to her. "Come along. I'll show you."

She let him pull her to her feet and then she followed him to his cabin. Captain Aragon's cabin was the grandest on the ship, and though most of the ship was exquisitely designed, she had never imagined that his quarters would be so beautiful. His suite was quite large, and it had a big full bathroom, as well as a private study with a small library, and a nook for breakfast or tea. It looked out over the back of the ship, and he even had a private deck there that he could walk out on.

He went to the bedside table at the near side of his bed and picked up a picture frame, gazing at it in silence with a stoic face before handing it to Jules without looking at her.

Inside the frame was a photograph of her Aunt Vianne and Kadian, standing on a white sandy beach together, their arms around each other, with grins on their faces.

"Is that the island where the ship was docked in the hidden lagoon inside the cave?" She asked, seeing that it looked slightly familiar.

"Yes. That's my island. She visited me there often." He answered quietly. "That was a while back. We were in love, but we couldn't be together." He sank down into a sumptuous armchair and lifted one hand to his temple, rubbing his fingertips over it as he stared off into nothing. "I was a time pirate." He said in a low voice. Jules mouth fell open.

"I couldn't tell her because I didn't want to lose her. There was a great battle between the Time Guardians and the pirates, and Marleigh was killed in the battle. I was there. I didn't know the Starling sisters would be there, but they had worked hard and figured out enough to try to stop the pirates, they showed up with several other guardians, and the battle ensued. They'd finally found us. I fled the battle the moment I found out that they were there; I didn't want them to see me and find out what I was. I couldn't let my love know that I was a time pirate. Then I heard that Marleigh had been killed, and that was too much for me. I left the time pirates for good." He closed his eyes and pressed the fingertips of one hand to his forehead, as if he was attempting to stem an oncoming headache.

Jules could not believe what she was hearing. She was totally floored and nearly speechless.

"Then Vianne went missing, and I knew that she was taken by the time pirates. I vowed to get her back and kill the Commodore for what he'd done to them; exact my revenge on him, and save Vianne." He opened his eyes and looked at Jules.

"I left the time pirates for many reasons. The killing of Time Guardians is unforgiveable in the Universe, aside from the fact that I'm still in love with Vianne." He shook his head. "It just wasn't what I signed up for."

Rising from his chair, he began to walk slowly around the room, running his hand lightly over the things that he passed. "I had been making this ship for a long while, building it in the cave on my island, finding just the right crew for it. We were ready, when I left the time pirates, we were ready to go, and it was a good thing that we were, because that's when Vianne disappeared."

Jules frowned. "How can that be? How did you do it all so fast?"

He turned his gaze to meet hers. "Time moves at different speeds in different places. When I left the pirates, I had a year of earth time with me. I stole it from them. I used that year all at once to finish the ship, hire and train the crew, and we were about to leave when Sprocket, who Marina had stationed at the Time Palace, told us that you and Henry were there, and who you were. We went straight to Ramblewood to get you, as soon as Sprocket told us you were leaving the palace."

The young girl nodded and pushed her hands down into the pockets of her robe. "I understand." She cocked her head to one side then. "Since you were a time pirate, don't you know where they are?"

He shook his head. "The time pirates are doing some of the dirtiest work ever done in the universe, stealing time, and those in charge are being very careful about who they let get close to them. When I left them, I hadn't been with them long enough to learn where the fleet docks. I hadn't earned their trust or that right of knowledge by that point. You see, there is a whole fleet out in space, stealing time from many places, not just Earth. I was in the fleet. When a mate is in the fleet long enough, and works hard enough, and earns the trust of the Commodore, then that mate is moved to one of the three command ships. They are great and mighty ships. All of the other ships that the fleet uses are just runner ships. They only dock at space ports as they go along stealing time. None of the runner ships ever go to the stronghold; the secret base, to dock."

Jules took a few steps toward him, closing the distance between them. "Do you think we'll get her back?" She asked, hope and doubt and anxiety all whirling in her head and heart. She had known he had secrets, but she never would have guessed at what he'd told her.

His eyes flashed and he pushed his chin out. "I will not stop until I get her back."

Jules gave him a nod. "We won't stop either. We'll work with you to do whatever it takes, and we will get her back."

Kadian blinked and then gave her a smile. "You know, it's a little while before breakfast still. You could go back to your cabin and try to get some rest if you like. You said you didn't sleep well. Maybe now you could get a nap in while you have a chance."

Jules thanked him and left, her mind dizzied with all that she had learned. When she opened the door to her cabin, she saw that Finn and Henry were both awake. Henry vaulted from his bed and reached his hand to her arm.

"I'm so relieved that you're okay! I was worried about you!" He let out a heavy breath and his shoulders drooped a little.

Her eyes were wide as she sat on her bunk and patted the space next to her for them to sit beside her. "I was out on the deck because I couldn't sleep, and while I was out there, Captain Aragon saw me and took me to his cabin to talk."

Finn and Henry looked surprised. "Were you in trouble? What did you two talk about?"

Jules couldn't even believe she was saying it. "He's going after the time pirates to rescue Aunt Vianne because he's in love with her!"

Both Henry's and Finn's mouths fell wide open.

"He showed me a photo of the two of them together on his private beach at his island where this ship was docked. It looked to me like she was pretty crazy about him, too!" Jules felt her cheeks flush a little at the thought of it.

Jules shared everything that she had heard with her brother and Finn, telling them how Kadian was once a time pirate, how he had stolen a year of time and finished the ship and found the crew. She told them how he had been in the battle where Marleigh was killed, and how he had left right away to avoid being seen by either of them. She told them everything, and they only stopped her with a question twice as they let her explain it all.

Finn shook her head in amazement. "The Time Guardians are still a mystery to me. I just don't understand it."

"It's still a mystery to me too." Henry admitted.

"Me too." Jules added. "I didn't learn much from the Empress, she just wasn't going to answer very many questions or tell me everything that I really wanted to know. I still have millions of questions about it all."

Henry brightened then with a grin. "Wait! Rastaban knows! He was going to tell me before he had to shrink down to travel size and sneak out of the palace with us." He ran over to the garden box he had made and found his fluffy rainbow bookworm friend munching on a leaf. "Will you tell us?" He asked, eyes shining.

"Of course! I'd love to tell you all about them." He seemed well pleased with his audience, and Henry took his seat on his sister's bunk again where they were huddled. He propped his knee up, and set Rastaban on it, so they could all see each other.

Rastaban drew himself up, looking a little larger as he did so, and cleared his throat. "To explain it all properly, I'll need to start at the beginning."

There was a soft whirring noise and they all turned to see the Sprocket teddy bear shifting into a cat. The cat jumped up on the bunk with the children, and sat alert, ears perked up, curious, ready and waiting to listen.

"A very long time ago, there was a star called Cerulean, because that was the color that it was; a beautiful blue. It was an anomaly in the Universe. No one had ever seen one like it before, and there has not been one since. It was a single star, and it went supernova; exploding and then cooling and shrinking. When it cooled, the core of the star hardened, as they do, but it did not harden into iron. It hardened into a glowing blue crystal, and the core of the star was mined." Rastaban looked at Jules then.

"Get your Cerellus."

She pulled it from beneath her robe and pajamas and he raised one fluffy brow at her. "Didn't the Empress give you a box to keep that in?"

"I'm not putting this in a box. It was my mother's, and I'm going to keep right on wearing it." she replied firmly. Then her tone lightened some as she looked at the worm. "I am being really careful with it, though."

Rastaban chuckled. "Well then carefully twist the eastern and western hemispheres of the globe in opposite directions."

Jules held the sphere delicately in her fingertips, and with the greatest wariness, she reached through the two metal rings that designated latitude and longitude, and she slid the brass sphere in opposite directions as Rastaban had instructed. It opened.

Inside was a glowing blue chip of a crystal. All three children breathed in and leaned closer for a better look at it.

The bookworm continued. "That chip was part of the star at one time, and that Cerellus is genetically linked through that special crystal, to your mother."

"Aunt Vianne has a similar necklace, but it's a little different." Henry added, examining it closely, but not touching it.

"All Time Guardians have a Cerellus, and each one is genetically linked to a Time Guardian. There are Time Guardians all over the Universe." Rastaban explained.

"Can anyone be a Time Guardian?" Finn asked, looking slightly hopeful.

Rastaban shook his head, and his feathery fringe swayed back and forth. "No. Only people with the right DNA can time travel with the Cerellus device."

Finn was disappointed. "I traveled with Jules and Henry from my home in New York in 1849, and that worked."

Henry frowned and scratched his head. "I still have no idea how it even happened in the first place."

Jules looked at the little worm. "Do you know how it works?" She asked curiously.

Rastaban was quiet and thoughtful for a long moment. "I do know. Very well, I'll tell you how it works, provided you do not make use of it traveling through time." He looked keenly at both Henry and Jules.

"We won't." Jules agreed grudgingly. Henry nodded his head as well.

"Time Guardians with a Cerellus have only to think of where they're going, and they go there, to that time and place. If they are thinking of the people they are with and touching them, then those people go as well."

Henry and Jules brightened then. "That's how Finn wound up traveling with us!" Henry was delighted to have the mystery solved. "I'd been reading about immigrants in that time era in a book that day for school." He gave his head a shake and he smiled. "I was still thinking of it when Jules and I were in the greenhouse looking for Aunt Vianne. I was going to tell her that I'd finished the book." His smile faded.

"There's quite a bit more to it, but that should be good for now. You'll learn the rest in time." Rastaban promised.

Just then there was a knock at the door. Henry rushed to put Rastaban in his pajama shirt pocket, and the worm ducked down. "Come in!" He called when it was safe.

Nicodemus poked his grey head around the corner and gave them all a smile. "I wanted to let you know that breakfast is about to be served. You'll want to hurry to the Wardroom."

The children scrambled off of Jules' bunk to get ready, and Nicodemus nearly left before he poked his head back in one more time. "Oh, Henry, that little worm you've been carrying around… Rastaban, he is welcome to join us if he likes." He gave them a wink.

All three children stared at him with wide eyes and open mouths. He closed the door and left them.

"How'd he know?" Henry whispered, checking to see if Rastaban was fully covered by his pocket.

As the children were seated at breakfast, Jules spoke up and directed a question to Kadian at the head of the table.

"Captain, what is the Port of Morrow like?" She, Henry, and Finn had been speculating, but as none of them had ever been to a space port, none of them had any real idea about what it would be like.

"It's a larger port, about the size of a small moon where ships on galactic trade routes stop for refueling, commerce, jobs, entertainment, vacation, and sometimes illegal dealings." He answered, telling her most of it.

All three children shared eager looks with each other. "We're so excited to see it!" Finn exclaimed with delight.

"I'm sorry, but you can't come into the port with me. I must pretend to be a time pirate again so that I can find out if anyone knows where they are. August will be posing as the Captain of the ship while I hope to slip off of the ship unseen and onto the docks. For this endeavor, I cannot be associated with this ship if I'm to be believed in the port. The other officers are going into the port for supplies, and you certainly can't go into port alone. I am sorry about it." He gave them a sympathetic look.

Jules, Henry, and Finn felt as if every bit of happiness and air had deflated from them, and they all looked down at their plates, utterly disappointed.

James, who was serving the head end of the table at that moment, looked down at Jonathon, who was serving the opposite end, and he raised his voice slightly. "We could take the children into port with us; Jonathon and me. It wouldn't look suspicious if they were kitchen hands, and we could probably use their help, to be truthful."

Jonathon looked at the children and saw rays of hope beaming from their lifted faces. "Yes, I think that would be a fine idea, if the children and you agree, Captain." He looked over at Kadian.

"Yes, I think that would be fine. They go with you both then." Kadian gave a nod and the children tried to hold in a squeal of excitement as they went back to their meals.

Trinity was seated next to Finn, and she leaned over and spoke to all three of them. "Corliss, Shakti, Tendaji, August, and the Captain will need to be at their posts as the ship is brought into port, but Paisley, Nicodemus, Samuel, and I would be glad to have you up on the deck with us so that you can watch as the ship comes into port. What do you think?"

Finn nearly bounced in her seat. "Yes! Thank you!"

Henry and Jules felt just the same about it, and thanked Trinity as well. They were all thrilled to be seeing something new and exciting like the space port.

When breakfast was finished, Jonathon and James sent the children to their cabin to ready for the venture, rather than helping the kitchen ratings with the dishes.

"What do you think it will be like?" Finn asked, tugging her clothes and shoes on.

"I don't know." Jules reflected on it, brushing her hair thoughtfully and pulling it into a ponytail. "We've seen so many Hollywood space movies that have space ports, and they're all different. I have no idea what it will be like."

Henry came out of the closet with his clothes on and sat in the chair near the sofa. "I think there will be a lot of ships there, and people. Perhaps the ships will be different than this one, and I'm not sure if all of the people will look like us. I was thinking about the Empress and how she looks a little different. It would be presumptuous of us to think that all life in the Universe looks like us as humans." He smiled then and looked at the other two. "It's really quite exciting, isn't it?"

"It is!" Jules agreed.

Finn sat down on the sofa near Henry and Jules sat with her and brushed her hair for her. Finn toyed with the hem of her pants, running her fingers back and forth over it as she spoke quietly.

"I'm a little scared." She admitted.

"Of what?" Jules asked, leaning around the girls' shoulder to look at her face.

"What if I get lost there, and the ship leaves without me? What if I never find my way back to you again, or Earth? What if I'm lost in outer space?" She looked up at Henry and Jules then and they could see that she was genuinely afraid of what could happen.

Henry shook his head and planted his palms on his knees as he looked at her. "Well first of all, I don't think the ship would leave without you, and second, James and Jonathon will take good care of us. They'll make sure we're safe. Even so, let's make a promise that we will stay together so that no matter what happens, we won't get lost. Right?" He proposed.

"Right. We stick together." Jules agreed.

A smile of relief came over Finn's face. "Right."

Jules stood up then and looked at Henry and Finn. "I think we're ready. Let's head up to the deck."

Henry made sure that Rastaban was tucked safely into his shirt pocket, and he rose from the chair. "Ready." He said. Finn grinned and joined them.

Sprocket shifted from a teddy bear into a hawk, and he flew along with the children as they headed up to the deck.

Chapter Nine

~

The Port of Morrow

When they reached the deck, Trinity and the others were waiting for them. She waved at them and they joined the group at the front of the ship to watch the port come into view.

"I have these for you!" Trinity told them, handing each of them a shoulder bag. "Just in case you want to pick anything up in the port to bring with you back onto the ship."

The children examined their soft, dark brown shoulder bags happily, pulling the flap open and peering inside of them before putting them on and adjusting them.

"Thank you!" Jules' eyes shone as she spoke to Trinity. Henry and Finn thanked her as well.

"I've got these for you." Paisley told them, handing each of them a clear disk the size of their palms. The disks were thin and extremely light. She was, as always, wearing purple, though it was in a more violet shade that day, in pants and a jacket.

"What is this?" Henry asked, turning the disk over in his hands.

Nicodemus answered. "It's called Verito. It's money. You see, different assets vary in value across the Universe. On Earth, precious metals and gemstones carry great value, but in other worlds, they really aren't worth much. There are desert worlds where water is the greatest asset. There are worlds where electronics bring the most value. Some worlds are always cold, like winter, so fresh food and heat producers are considered the most valuable. In order to trade across all worlds, all the active worlds in the Universal Alliance agree to the use of credits, and people trade them for goods or services. The credits are used like money and they are kept on the Verito disks."

He showed them a little digital display on one side of their disks. "Your disks each have thirty credits. When you touch the disk this way, you can arrange a transfer of credits. Let's do this, each of you transfer five credits to the other; Jules to Henry, Henry to Finn, Finn to Jules."

The three children touched their disks and transferred five credits to each other. Nicodemus smiled widely at them.

"Well done! Now you each still have thirty credits, and you've learned how to use your Verito disk. You're ready!" He looked as though he was proud of them as he stood back up and watched them.

Jules laughed softly. "I guess Earth must not be an active world in the Universal Alliance."

Samuel shook his head. "There are some ships based off of Earth, but officially no. Earthling humanity is not yet at a state of maturity when they could be approached and welcomed into the Universal Alliance. They have a long way to go before they get to that point." He sounded a little disappointed about it.

The group of them stood at the railing and the children watched with wide eyes as the Port of Morrow came into view and the ship began to slow down on approach.

Captain Aragon had been right; it was the size of a small moon with a massive city covering most of it. Henry, Jules, and Finn stared in fascination as many different kinds of ships flew around them, in and out of the port. The traffic wasn't thick, but it was more than the children had expected. Some of the ships were smaller and some larger. Most were made of some kind of metal, though there were a few others that were made of materials similar to that of the Gypsy Windlass. Some looked like space ships, some like airships, some like sailing ships.

Finn screwed up her face slightly. "Why are there so many different kinds of ships?" She asked curiously.

Paisley rested her hand on the girls' back. "They're all made on different kinds of worlds, and people use the materials and technology that they have at hand."

Finn nodded at her and then forgot all about her question as the ship neared the dock. They could see a thick concentration of tall buildings which were separated by avenues, though some vehicles were driving along the avenues, and most other vehicles were flying up in the air above the avenues. There were many people, and strange creatures, and all of it looked very busy.

Trinity leaned closer to them and spoke gently. "As the Ship's Culturalist, I want to remind you that you're going to see a lot of aliens in this port, and you mustn't stare. It's rude. I understand that you might be surprised by some of them, but be polite and smile. Don't wave. Stay close to Jonathon and James, and you'll be fine."

They all three promised her they'd be on their best behavior. Jonathon and James walked across the deck toward them then, and the children were surprised to see them dressed in travel clothes, rather than kitchen or serving attire.

The ship pulled up against the dock, swaying slightly, and then there was a soft jolt, and the ship was still.

August Holt came out of the Bridge and walked down the center of the deck, looking every part the Captain of the ship. Kadian was nowhere to be seen.

Paisley, Samuel, Trinity, and Nicodemus said goodbye, and followed August off of the vessel to the port.

Jonathon and James turned to the children and smiled. "Let's be off, shall we?" James gave his head a turn to the pier, and the children followed him, with Finn holding tightly to Jules' hand. Sprocket flew just over their heads, staying with them, his hawk eyes keeping a good view of what was going on all around.

The first sensation that the children had about the pier was that it was noisy and hectic. Machines hummed and whirred on the pier and the space ship engines roared at a slight distance. Pier workers and ship crews talked and yelled and bartered and argued in pairs and groups all over the docks. The city that loomed up behind them had a cacophony of its own noises, some seemingly familiar, others strange.

Aliens in a wide array of colors, shapes, and sizes walked, crawled, shuffled, and flew everywhere that the children looked, and they tried hard not to stare as Trinity had instructed them.

The space station was all machine, and the lighting over the whole of it was bright, but not warm like sunlight. The air was artificial, pumped through great machines at intervals throughout the station, cleaned, and pushed out into the port again.

Finn turned her head from one side to the other, taking it all in, and then she looked at Henry and Jules. "It's strange here."

"It is." Henry agreed.

"I think it's really interesting." Jules replied as she gazed at it in fascination.

"I don't mind it for a wee bit, but I wouldn't want to stay here for long." Finn determined.

They walked off of the docks and onto the first two avenues nearby. There were shops lined up side by side all down the road, all of them a little dirty and looking banged up, as if they had seen better days and never would see them again.

"Watch and learn, and do not speak while we're in these first few places." Jonathon told the children. They agreed. Sprocket folded his wings and stood at attention on James' shoulder, spying everything.

The two men took them into the first shop, where a creature who somehow resembled both a frog and a fish was standing on two thick legs and wearing clothes that didn't quite fit him. His dark green, beige, and pale white colored figure was large, spilling out where his clothes did not quite cover his body.

He eyed them all closely when they walked in; his great glassy fish eyes appearing to see everything about them.

The creature's wide mouth opened, and he spoke to Jonathon and James, who began to discuss a purchase of some of the meats that were sold in the shop. At the front of the store where they'd come in, there were dried meats for sale, next were freezers with glass doors filled with frozen meats, and just a bit further back, there were cages chock full with some of the strangest animals and birds the children had ever seen, and none of them were from Earth. 'Fresh Meat'. Read the sign over the cages. The children blinked in horror and turned, going straight back to the front of the store to wait for the men. When their orders had been placed and the dealing was done, James and Jonathon led the children back out onto the street and they walked a short distance to the next shop.

It seemed that most of the shops along the avenue where they walked were businesses where stores and provisions or useful machines and parts could be purchased for all of the ships coming in to the port. They shopped for all manner of food stuffs from ingredients to packaged products. They bought meats and cheeses, breads and cakes, some vegetables and fruits; some of which the children had never seen, spices and concoctions, and a variety of drinks to be stored on the ship.

The children had seen the pantry just off of the kitchen more than once by that point, and they knew how full Jonathon liked to keep the shelves. James also refilled the wine cellar from two of the shops on the road. Everything that was purchased was to be delivered to the ship immediately, so that while the men and children spent their time purchasing goods from the merchants, they carried nothing with them save for a few small bags of things the men had picked up along the way.

At last James and Jonathon turned to the children when they'd left the last shop. "We've got all the supplies we need, so now let's take you three into the city center to get a look there."

The children felt a rush of excitement and anticipation as the men led them away from the dockside streets and into the heart of the Port of Morrow. Sprocket unfolded his wings and flew just above their heads again as he kept watch over them.

Strange sights awaited them there. Small air pods flew all around, hovering and zipping about, carrying people as they came and went on their way. There were street merchants lined up almost shoulder to shoulder, selling everything that one could imagine, crying out to passersby, peddling their wares.

They saw jars made of different materials in many sizes, which smoked, and Jules sniffed the air and asked Jonathon if it was incense.

"Some of the smoke in incense. It's best not to breathe it in. Let's keep going." He gave her a pat on the shoulder and they continued onward.

They saw snake charmers who played on unusual flutes, making the snakes dance and float. There were street merchants offering perfumes, waving their bottles of scent just under the noses of people passing by, but James and Jonathon pulled the children close between them and waved the perfume sellers away.

"It's not always perfume that they're selling." Jonathon advised. "Sometimes it's a sleeping mist that takes hold a minute or two later, when you're just a short way down the road here, and you fall asleep, and they have a friend drag you off to a dark corner to go through your pockets and leave you there."

The children's eyes grew wide with a little fear and wonder, and they felt wiser knowing the truth about the possibility of danger around them.

"Kind of like the mist or smoke that surrounded us at Ramblewood?" Jules asked, shooting both men a suspicious look.

"Was it black? Made a cloud and you couldn't see?" Jonathon asked.

"Yes." All three children answered.

He chuckled softly. "Ah. That was Marina's work. She invented a sleeping mist of her own design. Had to get you onto the ship, I suppose."

Just then they passed a booth all hung about with silks, and the merchant rushed out and wrapped a long swath of dark sea green silk around Jules. "This is perfect for you! It brings out your eyes! This is the finest silk you'll find in the Universe! It's not cheap, but I will give you a good price for it, just for you, because I like you." The merchant beamed at her.

"Are you shopping for silks?" James asked, looking down at Jules. She liked the look and feel of the silk, but she shook her head.

"I'm not looking for silk today." She smiled at the merchant and he tried to press her further about it, but James stepped in between them, his broad and solid body forming a wall as he walked Jules away from the booth.

Just down the road from the silk merchant was a booth filled with small animals, and Finn was delighted with the peculiar little creatures. Some had a head, two arms and hands, and one tail, some had short round bodies with small feet and hands, some were long with rows of hands and feet, almost like a caterpillar.

Jonathon asked Finn if she was planning on getting a pet, and he told her that if she did get one, she would be responsible for caring for it. She hesitated.

"I do want one, but I don't know where I'll be. I hope I'll be at Vianne's home, but right now nothing is certain. I'd rather wait until I have a home to live in before I get a pet. I wouldn't want a life on the run for these wee ones." She gave the creatures a pat and a smile, waving at the kindly merchant, and they walked on.

Henry and Jules exchanged a heartfelt look. They both wished that Finn felt as if her life was more stable, but they knew she was right.

A few paces more down the street and Henry found a booth selling a wide range of toys the likes of which were strange to the children. They stopped to look, and Henry discovered one that intrigued him.

The merchant showed him how they worked. "This ball fits right in your palm." He said, placing on in each of the children's hands. "Now, stand apart from each other." He told them, and the children walked away from one another.

"Touch the button on the ball." He called to them, and they did. Jules' ball lit up and turned a pretty shade of blue. Henry's ball lit up green, and Finn's ball lit up yellow. "Now, walk toward each other!" The merchant told them. They did so, and the closer they got to one another, the brighter the lights in the balls glowed. When they were within a couple of feet of each other, the colors in their balls began to change and swirl, Henry and Finn were closer together than Jules was to them, and their balls both swirled with yellow and green light, then when Jules reached them, each ball swirled with yellow, green, and blue light.

"They are perfect for hide and seek!" The merchant encouraged them. "I activate them at purchase and they are guaranteed to last always!"

Henry and Jules walked backward again, watching as the distance between them made the light in the balls change, so that they were only their own color again, and the further they went, the dimmer the light became. As they came closer together again, the lights grew brighter, swirling with each other's colors once more.

Looking up at the merchant, Henry gave him a nod. "We'll take them." He moved his finger over the Verito and transferred fifteen credits to the merchant, buying all three balls for them.

"Thank you!" Finn bubbled with joy.

"Thanks Henry!" Jules reached her arm around him and hugged his shoulders.

"Now we will be able to find each other, if we need to." Henry told them with a smile. They all three hugged one another, and James and Jonathon told them it was time to go back to the dock.

They stopped at one more shop along the way, and Jonathon bought them each a small bag of candy from the candy merchant, which they were delighted with.

When they reached the dock, James and Jonathon stopped at the planks where the loading bay on the ship was joined to the dock, to check their stores and supplies orders. They were talking with the merchants and delivery people when Finn tugged silently at Henry and Jules' sleeves.

She jerked her head to one side and they followed her eyes to a spot a short distance away. Henry whispered. "Kadian!"

The Captain looked every bit a pirate, and he was headed straight for a surly looking fellow. Jules turned to the others. "Do you want to go see what he's doing?" She asked, knowing she shouldn't.

Henry looked over his shoulder. James and Jonathon were both in deep conversation with those they were talking to about their orders.

"We'll go and be right back. We'll be fast. They'll never miss us." Henry answered; a spark of adventure in his eyes. Finn nodded eagerly, and the three of them slipped away quietly, as Sprocket flew silently over their heads, guarding them.

They hid behind a stack of crates, listening in as Kadian spoke with the surly man. The man shook his head and waved his hand in the air. "I don't know who you're talking about. I never heard of them, and I never seen a ship like the ones you asked about. Get out of here and be on your way. No one here likes your kind!"

Kadian lifted his chin and looked the man dead in the eye. "Oh I think you do know, and you're going to tell me where I can find them, because if you don't, you'll wish with terror saturating every bone in your body that you had."

"Don't you threaten me!" the heavy man snarled, reaching for his knife.

"Ah… ah… ah… mustn't touch that." Kadian told him evenly. With a casual air, he dipped his gloved fingers into a pocket on his jacket and he pulled out a black pocketwatch and showed it to the man. The big man's rough and tumble appearance disintegrated upon sight of the small black time piece.

"I'll suck your whole life away with this. You won't even have time to take your next breath." Kadian didn't so much as blink as he stared cold and hard at the man.

Henry looked over at Jules and whispered. "Did you know he had that? What is it?"

Jules shook her head. "No, I didn't know he had that, but he was a time pirate, wasn't he? Maybe that's what they use to steal time. Sounds like it, doesn't it?"

Henry shrugged, and they turned their eyes back to the Captain.

The big man began to blubber and sputter, stepping back away from Kadian and holding his hands up in the air. "I didn't know! I didn't know you was one of 'em! Don't steal any time from me! Please!"

"Have you seen any of my friends?" Kadian took a couple of steps toward the man.

The heavy man quivered and nodded. "Yeah, I do know of one. They was all here in their ships, just like you said. They was stealing time from so many. They left, and there was one of them who stayed behind."

"Where is he?" Kadian demanded with an icy voice.

"He's... he's in the pub; *The Time Bandit*, just across the way there!" the man was trembling and backing up away from the Captain.

Kadian's hand shot out and he grabbed the man by the dirty stained collar of his shirt, hauling him closer. "You'd better forget you ever saw me."

The man nodded adamantly, and when Kadian turned him loose, he ran fast. Kadian straightened his jacket and headed for *The Time Bandit*.

The children followed at a short distance, fascinated with what they were discovering. Finn found a dark corner near an alley for them to hide in where they could watch the door of the pub. They knew they couldn't go into it, but they could get close. Sprocket stayed above them, eyes on everything.

Not two minutes later, the door was flung open so hard that it crashed against the wall behind it, and Kadian strode out dragging a scraggly looking man out by the back of his collar.

"Shady, I should have known it was you!" Kadian growled menacingly.

The man called Shady flailed and protested weakly, but Kadian hauled him all the way back to the ship and the children followed.

They hadn't gotten ten feet when suddenly dark cloth closed all around them, and they were hoisted up off of the ground. They were in sacks; Jules in one, and Henry and Finn in another.

They kicked and screamed, wriggling all that they could, but to no avail. "Henry! Finn!" Jules cried out, her throat tightening and tears stinging at her eyes as fear gripped her heart.

"Jules! I can hear you!" Henry called back. "Finn's with me! We've been taken!"

"Me too!" Jules shouted back, her blood racing as she tried desperately to get free.

"The lot of you, shut it!" Came the deep voice of a man. "Keep it up and we'll beat you!"

Jules' eyes were wide in terror. She wasn't with Henry and Finn, and she could do nothing to protect them if they were in danger of being beaten. She realized that at that moment, silence was her only option. Even the thought of either of them being beaten gave her the chills. She stopped struggling and sat silent, thinking of anything that might get them out of their predicament.

Sprocket screamed out with a metallic hawk's cry, and each of the children felt slightly better, knowing he was nearby. Henry held Finn in a hug. "Maybe Sprocket can get help from the ship. He knows where we are. We're going to be okay." He whispered to her. She stayed silent.

There was a loud metal thud, and then the cloth sacks were set down roughly on a hard metal floor. Jules' bag was opened first. She saw the other bag there, and knew that Henry and Finn were in it. They were in a pod bay, where one air pod was sitting on the metal floor nearby, and the area they were in was where another air pod would be. The bay door was metal, and Jules knew that it was how they had gotten in, and it was the door she had heard thudding when it was shut.

There were two men in space pirate outfits, who grabbed her and sat her down in a chair, tying her to it.

"You're never going to get away with this!" She growled angrily at them.

They ignored her and went to the second bag. She remembered what they'd said about hurting her brother and Finn, and she said nothing more. Henry and Finn were taken from the sack, both fighting and wrestling to get away.

Out of nowhere there was a loud bang on the bay door, and all of them gasped in surprise. The tall, skinny, brown haired pirate looked worriedly at the shorter, smaller, scruffy looking blonde haired pirate. "Wot was that?"

"I dunno." The blonde pirate answered, tying cords around Henry's hands behind his chair. The banging persisted.

"Maybe someone wants in?" The brown haired pirate suggested.

"So? If they come in, we'll kill 'em, right Ferdie?"

The brown haired pirate nodded.

The blonde haired pirate chuckled as he finished off Finn's cords behind her chair. "The Commodore is goin' to be right pleased to get the three o' you."

"You don't have to tell 'em everythin', Ox!" Ferdie glared at him.

"Why not? Maybe it'll scare 'em a bit. We can 'ave some fun with these kids 'afore we send 'em off to the big man." Ox laughed again.

Finn looked from one to the other of them and lifted her chin defiantly. "I don't know who this Commodore person is you're talking about, but I'll tell you this right now. Our father is a wealthy businessman and we're all here in port for a business meeting he's doing. We was let out to play on the docks while he's busy with his meeting, but if we're not back with him when it's done, the devil's comin' for you! He's a big shot, he is. If we aren't back with him when we're supposed to be, he'll be on the authorities right fast, and it'll be the sorriest mistake you ever made! I don't know what kids you think we are, but we ain't the ones you want. Your Commodore is goin' to be mighty put out if you bring him the wrong kids!"

Jules and Henry shared a look of wonder for a split second, and then Henry jumped right in with Finn. "My sister's right. You've had it if we aren't back with our father when we're supposed to be. You'll be arrested!"

Jules chimed in as well. "He's one of the most important businessmen on this whole port! You two are going to be in so much trouble! You have no idea who you've just grabbed!"

It bolstered their confidence to be bouncing their lies off of each other, hoping to sound believable.

Both of the pirates looked at each other and laughed.

Ferdie leaned down and placed his hands on his knees, looking at the children at eye level. "Nah, we know who you are, see, the Commodore has friends who told him about you. You're the Starling children, and no one knew you existed, but someone squeaked, and now everyone knows. There's a high price in the 'verse for the capture of you. We're gonna turn you in to the Commodore. We'll be the best of the bunch!"

Ox laughed and nodded, and then stopped and looked at Ferdie. "Wait a minute now."

Ferdie blinked. "What?"

Ox furrowed his blonde brow and scratched his scraggly hair. "You know, mercenary is really a step up from pirate, isn't it? Maybe we should think about sellin' 'em to the highest bidder. You know, make some real money. If these kids is really that valuable, we could make a fortune and then retire. No more working for that terrifying Commodore." He gave Ferdie an encouraging nod.

Ferdie blinked and thought about it. The banging on the metal bay door persisted relentlessly.

"Oh alright, if you think we could get some real money, give it a go. We split everything fifty-fifty, though."

Ox nodded. "I know who I'm going to start with. Probably no one wants those kids more than Asterisma!"

Ferdie shuddered. "She's much worse than the Commodore!"

"I only care about the money." Ox said with a half toothless smile. He pulled out a hand held machine with a small monitor and ran his finger over the screen. Moments later the children heard a cold and cruel sounding voice answer.

"Asterisma! I can't believe I found you!" He turned to his friend then. "Look Ferdie, I found her!" Turning back to the monitor, he continued. "Listen… I got the sweetest deal you ever heard of." Ox began, grinning crazily at the screen.

"How dare you contact me! I am not buying anything!" She snapped at him.

Ox just smiled coolly. "Would you be interested in three Starling children what have been kept secret all their lives?"

There was silence at the other end for a moment, and the children all looked at each other in confusion and surprise.

"That's not possible!" Asterisma sounded highly annoyed. "There are no Starling children!"

"Yeah? Take a look." Ox turned his device around and the children could see that it was a two way camera. The woman on the screen before them was tall and willowy, with extraordinarily pale skin and long thin graceful hands. Her long black hair hung down around her narrow face, framing her violet eyes.

"This one's got a Cerellus." Ox continued, going to Jules and pulling her pendant out from her vest. She wiggled in her chair to stop him, but to no avail.

"Put that down! Don't you touch that!" Jules fired at him.

"There's only the one Cerellus, but there is three of these Starling kids here." Ox grinned at Asterisma.

"That's incredible!" The woman replied coldly. "It's no surprise that my sister kept them a secret." She was quiet a moment as an evil grin spread over her face. "What a treasure. It was right of you to contact me. I want them. I want all three of them, and the Cerellus. I will pay any price for them. Even a million. Get them to me here at my palace, and I will give you a million credits for them."

Ox swallowed and lifted his chin bravely. "The Commodore wants them just as bad as you do. We could give 'em to him instead."

"Name your price!" She demanded. "I'm desperate! I need them!"

"One million credits… each." Ox stated, his hands trembling and his face flushing red as he spoke.

She didn't hesitate. "Fine. Do it. Bring them to me and I'll pay you a million credits each for them. I want them here as soon as possible!"

"They are yours. We're on our way." Ox said, and ended the call.

Ferdie jumped in the air and whooped for joy. "You did it! We're gonna be rich now!"

The banging on the door grew more persistent and louder, never stopping.

"We gotta get these brats there first. Come on now. Help me load them into the crate." Ox told him with a grin.

The children looked at each other in horror. As each one was untied, they were pushed into a medium sized wooden crate. Jules couldn't stand up straight in it, and neither could Henry, they had to bend over or squat in order to fit.

The banging on the pod bay door was thunderous and incessant, and Ox finally screamed out. "I can't take that banging anymore! I'm gonna open that door and kill whoever it is that's been making all that racket!"

The children screamed and yelled for help, and though they fought as much as they could, they remembered what the pirates had said about beating them, and they were worried for Finn.

Finn wrestled Ferdie as much as she could, twisting and turning, climbing and squirming all over him as he fought to get her from the chair to the crate, but finally he got her into it.

Just then Ox opened the bay door, and Sprocket flew in, zooming around the room once before he spied the children in the wooden crate. He aimed right for it and zipped inside.

The moment he was in the crate, Ferdie slammed the wooden cover over it and sealed it. He laughed out loud. "We shut that thing up, didn't we? I guess Asterisma is going to get an extra little gift along with these kids."

"What the heck kind of bird was that?" Ox asked curiously.

"I don't know, but that's her problem, not ours." Ferdie answered. "We're going to give her the crate, collect our millions, and leave."

Ferdie and Ox moved the crate outside, and the children held on tightly to each other inside the wooden box.

"Where are we going?" Finn asked breathlessly.

"I don't know. They're taking us to someone called Asterisma. She looks so familiar, but I know I've never seen her before." Henry answered.

"I done something bad." Finn admitted with a small smile.

"What did you do?" Jules asked, looking at her in surprise. There were tiny shafts of light that filtered in through the crevices at the corners of the box, and through the small airholes along the panels of wood.

"When I was fightin with that pirate, I sneaked this off of his neck. He didn't even feel me take it. He won't ever know where he lost it." She held up a black pocketwatch exactly like the one that Kadian had showed the burly man on the docks.

Rastaban gasped. "Finn Murphy! You put that thing away right now and don't you get it out again. I strongly suspect that that's what the time pirates use to steal time! You be careful with that!"

Henry held up his hand and grinned. "Good job. High five, Finn."

"What's high five?" She asked, looking at his hand.

Jules reached up and slapped his hand. "That's a high five. Five fingers up high in the air. It means good job. Well done. Congratulations."

Finn raised her hand and Henry gave her a high five. Finn giggled a little.

"Let's get this crate loaded onto the ship!" They heard Ox call out.

Sprocket looked at the children. "All of you, get back away from me as far as you can."

The children scooted back into the corner and scrunched themselves up as much as they could into a ball.

Sprockets wings began to expand quickly and his body changed faster than they had ever seen it. The two bird legs he had been standing on grew long and front legs appeared out of his chest. His head shifted and the front of his face grew long.

In seconds he transformed into a life size Pegasus, much bigger than the box they were all in, which caused him to erupt out of the crate, sending splinters of wood flying in every direction. He whinnied loudly and snorted, standing up on his hind legs as the children gaped at him.

Ferdie and Ox were only a few feet away from him, staring up at him in shock, frozen in place. Sprocket kicked each one of them in the heads with his front hooves, and as they were falling, he swung his wide metal wings around and clocked them both again, sending them flying unconscious to the ground among the shards of wood.

Looking back at the children who were still huddled behind him, he knelt down to the ground. "Get on! Let's get out of here!"

They raced to him and climbed on, with Jules in front, Finn behind her, and Henry at the back. They all clung to each other and to him. A metal saddle formed over his back, securing all of them inside the edges of it.

"I didn't know you could change into something this big!" Jules cried out with a huge grin on her face as she gripped him.

"Neither did I!" He answered back. "I had to try though. I had to save you!"

With that, he reared back slightly and flapped his wings, creating a powerful wind around them. A moment later, they were airborne, flying away from the debris on the ground, and heading for the ship.

Rastaban hung halfway out of Henry's shirt pocket, some of his many caterpillar-like bookworm feet holding on to the shirt, while several other feet were opened up into the air. He let his head go back as his fluffy rainbow fringe danced in the airstream. "Wahoooo!" He cried out in his deep voice. "Waaaaaaahooooooooo!"

The children laughed and each held up one hand, shouting out loud as well, loving the feel of flying on the back of a Pegasus.

They drew near to the ship and Pegasus Sprocket landed gently at a short distance from it. He knelt down and the children climbed off of him, all of them wide eyed with wonder and amazement.

"I think you've been in enough trouble today." Sprocket said, shifting back into a hawk. "Let's call this whole escapade a secret, shall we?"

Rastaban nodded, still a little winded and dizzy. "I agree." He sank slowly back down into the comfort of the pocket.

"Thank you!" The children chorused with gratitude. The last thing they wanted was to be in any kind of trouble on the ship. They began walking toward the plank, sighing with relief.

"Where've you been!" James grabbed them by the arms suddenly, and the children's hearts almost stopped in their chests. "This is no place to wander off! All kinds of bad things could happen to you in a place like this! Now get back on the ship!" He scolded them, chastising and lecturing them all the way back to the deck, and they knew they should have gotten into much worse trouble than that, so they said nothing.

When they reached the deck, they stopped short and stared. Kadian stood staunchly with his feet apart and his arms folded across his chest. To one side of him were Wilson Ryers, the Chief Warrant Officer and Master at Arms, Harley Silverstein, the Bosun, and Katsuro Kuang, barefoot and in his gi. The children had had enough time in lessons with him by that point that they knew Katsuro could end the time pirate's life in seconds.

Shady, the time pirate whom Kadian had just dragged onboard, was bound at the ankles and wrists, with his arms behind his back. Wilson Ryers was hauling him upward by the ankles on a rope that was hung over a wooden arm which stretched out over the far side of the ship. He hollered and pleaded, wriggling some, though it did him no good. Wilson gave the rope a twist and Shady spun around in a circle upside down, yelling out in protest.

The children were horrified, and gasped loudly. James and Jonathon each grabbed onto their shoulders and pulled them back a bit, bringing them in protectively.

"Where are the Commodore's ships, Shady!" Kadian shouted at him.

"I'm not going to talk, and you can't make me!" Shady cried out, looking as if he might throw up.

Kadian raised his hand and waved it dismissively. "Corliss, take the ship out of port into space, and when we are one light year out, drop him."

Corliss nodded as if Kadian had just asked him to do something as menial as pulling his hands from his pockets. "Yes, Sir. Immediately." He turned and headed for the Bridge.

"Wait! Wait!" Shady shouted to them desperately. "I'll talk! You bloody pirates! I'll talk!"

Kadian paused in his step, and then turned slowly and looked back over his shoulder at Shady. His voice was even, and cool. "Whatever you have to say better be worth your life, because if it isn't, your life is over."

Corliss stopped in his walk to the Bridge and waited.

Shady began to tremble and tried not to weep. "I know you're looking for the Commodore. I know you are. You shouldn't be, you should leave that devil alone and live out your life, but I know you're going to go after him!"

"Where is he!" Kadian demanded.

"The Commodore's command ships all dock in a place called Wraith." He blubbered pitifully.

Kadian took several steps toward the edge of the deck, his eyes on Shady who was still dangling off of the wooden arm over the port. "All three ships?" He pressed.

Shady's body turned slowly in a circle as he hung by his ankles. "No, all thirty of them. The runner ships and the command ships are all going there now." He moaned miserably.

If Kadian was surprised, he didn't show it. "Why?" His tone grew dangerous.

"I don't know. They came here. They had already stolen more time than you can imagine, but they stole even more, and then they left." He tried to look at Kadian as he twisted on the rope. "I only know that something big is coming."

Kadian narrowed his eyes and glared at Shady. "And you don't know what it is."

Shady shook his head and then looked as if he regretted doing it. His face was turning red from the blood that was draining down into it. "No, they marooned me before I found out."

"Why?"

"Because I wouldn't steal time from an old, dying woman. She reminded me of me mum. I couldn't do it. I failed the test. They was gonna kill me, but I gave 'em me own time to make up for it. Then they left, and I been here ever since. Trapped. I don't 'ave enough time to get nowhere else!" Shady sobbed for a moment.

Rastaban had poked himself up from Henry's shirt pocket. He spoke, and his voice was a big as it had been in the Universal Library at the Time Palace, filling the deck with its deep reverberations.

"What do you mean they're in Wraith? There's no place called Wraith that's in any star chart or charted area of the known universe!"

Nicodemus stepped forward. "Rastaban is correct." He gave the bookworm a nod.

"Oh, it's there alright." Shady interjected. "Wraith is a galaxy. It's made up of dark matter, see, invisible to the naked eye. That was the perfect spot for their stronghold. They call it Morden, that fortress of theirs, that's in Wraith. It's a little galaxy tucked right into the edge of a bigger one; a galaxy graveyard."

Henry frowned. "What's a galaxy graveyard?"

Rastaban answered him. "It's essentially a compost heap in the universe; a galaxy graveyard forms new galaxies out of dark matter. They're dangerous places. They're usually avoided at all costs."

Nicodemus spoke up loudly, facing Shady. "What is the name of the bigger galaxy that this Wraith is supposedly a part of?"

"The Atlas galaxy." Shady answered, trying to tug his hands free of the ropes that bound his wrists, and getting nowhere with his efforts.

Paisley was fascinated. "Is that possible?" She asked, looking over at Nicodemus.

"It's unthinkably far-fetched, but it's certainly not impossible…" Nicodemus considered it. "If all of the right circumstances were met… I suppose."

Kadian was watching them and listening closely. "Is it possible? Could that actually exist?"

Nicodemus and Paisley shared a deep look. "We're going to go find out right now." They turned immediately and headed for the Observatory.

Shady saw them leave and he cried out loudly. "Oy! That's all I know! Now I'm getting' an 'eadache! Let me go!"

Kadian turned and looked back at him. "You're certain that you don't know anything else?"

Shady grew frustrated. "No! I already told you everything! Except this… if you go after the Commodore and all of his mates, you're headed to your death! You'll never make it into Wraith or Morden alive, and you surely won't make it back out again!

You won't take him by surprise. He's got eyes everywhere!"

Kadian waved his hand, and Harley, Wilson, and Katsuro hauled Shady back in, dropping him unceremoniously onto the deck, and then untying him. The three of them escorted him off of the ship with strict instructions to keep his mouth shut.

Kadian, Corliss, Samuel, and the children, with Rastaban poked up out of Henry's pocket, all went into the Observatory. Nicodemus and Paisley were already working hard at finding the mysterious galaxy.

Nicodemus drew down a massive radio telescope from the wall and Samuel opened the cupola ceiling. They pointed the special scope toward the Atlas galaxy, searching, sending radio waves at what they could see through the scope. Paisley and Corliss were each stationed at different control panels, turning dials and knobs, flipping switches and checking gauges. Kadian, Rastaban, Sprocket as a hawk, and the children, watched and waited.

The team worked diligently, and suddenly Nicodemus cried out. "Aha! I found it! That's astounding!"

August had just entered the room, and he and Kadian went to Nicodemus whose face was pressed up against the end of the telescope. "What?" They asked anxiously.

Nicodemus pressed a button on the telescope and a large screen lit up on one wall, showing a live feed of what could be seen through the telescope. "There, at the edge of Atlas, in the halo, there's a distortion; an anomaly!"

Nearly everyone in the room asked, "Where?" It was almost a chorus.

Henry pulled his red laser pointer from his pocket and directed the pinpoint end of it onto the screen. "There! See there's a dark mass; no stars, no light, and there's a distortion of light around it. See how the light curves, like a lens around the edge, just barely."

Jules turned and looked at him in surprise, and she wasn't alone, most of the crew in the room was impressed with him.

"Just so!" exclaimed Nicodemus, well pleased. "Excellent work, Henry. That small mass we can't see is quite possibly a dark matter dwarf galaxy. It's fascinating!"

Finn planted her hands on her hips and frowned suspiciously. "Wait, we're looking at something we can't see? How are we doing that?"

Nicodemus explained. "Yes. See that faint ring of light with darkness at the center?"

"Yes." She answered doubtfully.

"That's called an Einstein Ring. The stars behind the dark matter galaxy shine light out, and when the light passes the dark matter galaxy, the galaxy's gravity makes the light bend around it and that creates the ring of light that we can see. That's an Einstein ring. We just can't see what's at the center of it. Think of a person standing in a dark room with a light bulb on behind them. You couldn't see the person, but you could see the outline of light around the edge of them, so you know the light is behind them, and you know the person is there because you can see their outline. We can't see the Wraith galaxy, but we can see the outline of light from the stars behind it."

Kadian spoke, his voice tense and firm. "We might not be able to see it, but we're going to go find it. Give us the coordinates for that dark dwarf galaxy. That's where we're going."

Nicodemus gave the Captain a serious look. "It's roughly four billion light years away."

The Captain didn't even blink. "Then we'd better find a deep Hollow."

"Yes, Captain." Nicodemus nodded.

Jules turned and looked at the group. "What's a Hollow?"

Paisley gave her a smile and an answer. "It's kind of like a pocket in space-time. They're used to travel long distances in a short amount of time in space."

Henry perked up. "Kind of like a wormhole?"

Paisley tipped her head thoughtfully. "Sort of. Imagine a grid around us as far as you can see in every direction, and think of the lines of the grid, now in all those straight lines, picture one spot where they warm and bend down or out from the rest of the lines, as if it was very hot there and the grid melted in that one spot. That's a Hollow, and they form, sort of bubbling out all over space. Some are deeper than others. We run a sort of radar over those imaginary grid lines in every direction and when we detect an irregularity in the reading that the sensors send back to us, we know there's a Hollow there. We send radar waves into it to test its depth. The deeper it is, the further we can go in space. We set our coordinates and dive in."

Samuel looked intently at the children. "They're dangerous though; we never know when or where they'll open up or close. If they're shallow or growing shallower, we know they're closing and we don't risk the jump. The belief is that if you enter one as it's closing, you become trapped in the pocket and you can't ever escape."

Henry was wide eyed and breathless. "What causes them?"

Samuel's brown eyes studied the boy as he taught him. "They're created by magnetic storms moving through space. Think of the Hollow as space lightning. Lightning doesn't strike in space, but if it did, this would be the equivalent of it. The power in the storms builds up and releases energy in the form of a magnetic pocket – a Hollow, that warps time and space. We have to set our instruments before we enter them because once inside it, everything is haywire until we come back out. The engine room and the ship is all made of steel, wood, brass, glass, copper, and crystal because those block out some of the magnetism. Steel works best, though. That's why the Engine Room and the Bridge are encased in it, otherwise the magnetic storms would cause a disruption that would disable the ship completely and probably permanently."

The children gazed in awe at Samuel. Corliss laughed a bit. "Well let's go find one, the Captain isn't going to wait for long."

They all went to the Engine Room together. The children sat and watched the machines and listened for the irregularity; any sound or shift in the radar readings that was different than the ones they could easily see and hear.

Finn jumped suddenly. "I heard one! I did!"

Samuel knitted his brow. "Did anyone else hear it?"

Everyone shook their head, and some of them spoke softly. "No."

Finn insisted. "But I did hear it! I did!"

Everyone listened again, and Samuel held up his hand. "Wait! Finn was right! I can hear it too. She found it!" Finn beamed excitedly, and Samuel gave her a pat on the back. Henry and Jules grinned and gave her a thumbs up, which she returned to them.

"Coordinates!" Corliss called out, putting the Bridge online with speaker and live video. "We've found it, I'm entering the coordinates! Go straight for it now, it's deep enough for us to get close to Atlas, and we want to hit it before it begins to grow shallow!"

The Captain steered the vessel directly toward the Hollow as Corliss and the engine ratings crew pushed the engine to go faster, giving them a speed boost that accelerated the ship toward their target.

Just as they were about to enter it, there was a thundering boom and the ship rocked. Everyone grabbed on tight to whatever was stable near them, though Corliss and Paisley both fell to the floor, and Henry tumbled from his chair. Tamsin was lucky and grabbed tightly to one of the support beams, saving her from hitting the wall. The chandeliers tinkled and shook, and everything that wasn't secured went flying and crashed.

"What is that?" Jules cried out, rushing to help Henry and to make certain that Rastaban was okay.

Corliss stood up and his face grew pale as he spoke in a solemn voice. "It was a hit on the ship. Everyone brace yourselves-" everything else he said was drowned out by the Captain, whose voice sounded fiercely over the intercom throughout the whole ship.

"We're under attack! Stations! Shields up!" He commanded. Everyone on the crew went directly to a station where they could work to protect the ship and battle the attacker. Samuel looked over at the children, who had taken their seats before the monitors. "Strap yourselves in, now!" He instructed, and then went to his own station.

Henry got his buckles fastened, and Jules was just working hers when the ship took another hit, rocking less violently than it had with the first hit. The crew stumbled, but held fast and worked feverishly.

"Gunnery and artillery crew to posts! Fire!" The Captain ordered through the intercom. "Corliss, get this ship through the Hollow *now*!"

The ship rocked again, but not from a hit; the gunnery crew were firing back on the attacker. Corliss and Paisley were both doing all that they could to rush the ship to the Hollow and dive into it.

Turbulence wrestled the ship in every direction as they entered the Hollow. Corliss hit the intercom button and called out to the Captain on the Bridge. "We're in! We're in the Hollow! Hold on!"

Finn cried out desperately. "I can't make this work! I don't know how this works!" She was still struggling with her buckles, and doing her best to hold on in her seat, her small body being flung from one side of it to the other as she grappled helplessly.

"Oh no!" Henry cried out. "She has no idea what seat belts are!"

Jules unfastened hers and pushed herself from her chair, struggling to get over to Finn. "I've got you, little sister, don't you worry! I'm coming! Just hold on!"

Finn's face was tear streaked, but she clamped her small hands down on the arms of the chair and gritted her teeth, holding on with all her might. Jules fought to reach her, but she finally did, and in moments she had the young girl strapped in. She was just turning to get back to her own seat when the ship took another solid hit amidst the turbulence, and everyone and everything went flying.

Jules lost her balance and her grip, tumbling backward toward the engine casing, rolling across the floor until she struck it hard, her head slamming against the steel base of it. Then everything went black.

A Note to The Reader

Dear Reader,

You have come to a twist in the story, for you see, the Hollow into which the Gypsy Windlass and her crew have sailed is a tricky, temperamental, unpredictable place. We were warned that all of the instruments and machinery don't work inside a Hollow, and that everything goes haywire. So it was told, and so it has happened.

The result of the interference from the Hollow is that this story has three possible endings. We are coming up on Chapter Ten, the last chapter of the book, but due to the chaos in the Hollow, the story has been jumbled. There are three versions of Chapter Ten, and only one of them is true. Until Book II of The Starling Chronicles is released and we learn the actual chain of events that happened, we must leave it up to you, dear reader, to determine which of these three chapters is the real and true Chapter Ten.

Good luck, and Safe Journeys

Dash Hoffman

Chapter Ten

~

Version One

"Jules! Jules!" It was Henry's voice that Jules heard, but she couldn't see him. She tried to call out to him, but somehow she couldn't find her voice. It was black all around her, and she knew it wasn't space because there were no stars, there was just blackness everywhere.

Something pressed against her arm and her hand, squeezing her hand gently. "Jules!"

She felt as if she was pushing hard against some unseen barrier, trying to break free of it. She could feel that Henry was nearby, but she couldn't find him. She pushed and searched for a way to him, and the darkness seemed to lift a bit. He called out to her again and she struggled harder, and the shadows faded gradually. Light took the place of the dark, and she could hear more clearly. There were voices around her that she didn't recognize, but closer than all of them was Henry's voice, and Finn's along with it.

Jules drew in a deep breath and pushed hard again, squeezing Henry's hand and then opening her eyes slowly.

He was sitting beside her as she lay in a bed. On her other side was Finn, and both of them were looking worriedly at her. Sprocket was sitting on a chair just behind Henry, in the shape of a dog; the faithful protector.

"Where am I?" She asked, trying to sit up. As she moved, she discovered that there were tubes connected to the veins in her arms, and in lifting her head, she began to feel a dull throbbing at the back of it.

"You're in the sick bay on the ship." Henry answered in a tight voice. She could hear the anxiety in his tone.

"What am I doing here? What happened?" She asked, blinking and looking around.

There were three other beds in the room, but all of them were empty. There were machines all over most of them secured to the walls, where there were monitors showing different charts and graphs, some of them changing and beeping. One of the medical crew was standing several feet away talking to Dr. Juric Van Pelt, the Chief Medical Officer.

"We went into the Hollow and were attacked by another ship. Captain Aragon says it was one of the time pirate ships. He thinks they heard about us at the Port of Morrow. Finn and I were thinking it might be those two pirates, Ferdie and Ox, but we didn't tell anyone that. You got out of your chair to help Finn with her seatbelts, and fell. There was a lot of turbulence and the ship took a hit from the attackers. You hit your head on the base where the engine is." He looked pained even speaking about it.

Jules blinked and tried to sort it all out in her head, but much of it seemed confusing to her. "Well where are we now? Did we make it out of the Hollow? What happened to the ship? What happened to the attackers?"

Henry placed a hand on her shoulder. "Maybe take a breath. The doctor said that you have to remain calm. You can't get excited or agitated for a bit while you heal. Don't worry, I'll tell you all of it."

Finn held Jules hand up to her cheek, pressing it there. "Thank you for helping me. I'm sorry you were hurt."

Jules gave her a smile. "I'm glad I could help you. I'm sorry about being hurt too. We should have known you wouldn't know what a seatbelt was or how to work one, let alone one with several buckles on it."

She looked back at Henry then, waiting expectantly.

He drew in a deep breath and raked his fingers through his somewhat tousled hair at the top of his head. "Okay. So, first, everyone made it through the attack and the Hollow okay. You were the only one who was hurt, but you weren't hurt too bad, and you're healing well. The doc says you'll be up and going again pretty soon; we just have to be mindful of you for a bit. You know, keep an eye on you. Sprocket, Finn, and I haven't left your side once."

Jules gave them a grateful smile. "Thank you all."

"We made it through the Hollow, but we were fighting the other ship the whole time. They were tough, and it was a bad fight, but we won. There's ah… there's nothing left of that ship or anyone on it." He raised his eyebrows a little and gave his head a shake. "Captain Aragon wasn't kidding when he said he assembled the best possible crew. Everyone worked really hard, and it seems like all of them were either protecting the ship, getting us through the Hollow, or taking out the other ship, and all three things got done pretty quickly."

He cleared his throat and continued. "The Gypsy Windlass was damaged in the battle."

Jules' eyes grew wide. "How bad?"

Henry sighed. "Bad enough. We are a bit crippled. Corliss, Tamsin, Marina, Shakti, and Tendaji all advised that we seek out some kind of sheltering place to repair the ship before we try to go any further."

"Where are we? Where did we come out when we left the Hollow?" Jules asked anxiously.

"We're on the far side of the Atlas galaxy, so we're close to the time pirate's stronghold in the Wraith galaxy, but we still have a bit of a distance to go to get there. Nicodemus found a small planet and moon where we're going to try to hide so they can repair the ship. We're headed there now." Henry gave her a smile.

"Do they think they can fix the damage?" Jules asked with concern.

Henry nodded. "Yes. They should be able to get it all fixed. Ironically, what we need is time." He gave a little hollow laugh.

His sister chuckled a bit, too. "You'd think that out of everyone on this ship, Kadian or you or I could come up with as much as we need!"

"Not without breaking rules." Henry said, glancing down at Rastaban, who was poked up out of his pocket and gave them a stern look.

Dr. Van Pelt came over to them then, with a stoic look on his face. "It seems our patient is awake. How are you feeling?" He asked, peering closely at her and shining a light into her eyes to check her pupils.

She blinked and looked up at him. "I'm okay. I have a headache, but otherwise I feel fine."

He put his hands around her head and felt carefully. "You have a bump at the back of your head where the impact hit. That swelling will go down. You could put some ice on it to help it go down faster. I've given you something for the pain, so it won't hurt so much."

"When can I get out of here?" She asked with moderate hope.

He examined the back of her head and then looked at her. "I think you'd be fine to leave in a few hours, but be very careful, and don't do anything strenuous for a day or two. You need to rest."

She nodded. "Thank you, doctor."

He handed her a small paper bag with three pills in it. "Take one of these at each meal. If your head begins to hurt worse, come back and see me."

She agreed and he left them. Looking back at Henry and Finn, she sighed. "So what am I going to do for the next three hours while I have to lay in this bed?"

Henry smiled. "Well, I thought we could watch a movie, since Finn hasn't ever seen one."

"Do they have movies?" Jules asked with a growing smile of surprise.

"They have all the movies." He answered happily.

"What's a movie?" Finn asked, looking from one to the other of the Starlings.

Three hours and one film later, Dr. Van Pelt released Jules, and she, Henry, and Finn went up to the Bridge to see what was going on.

Captain Aragon was steering the ship at the ship's wheel, and when he turned to look over his shoulder at the door, all three children could see relief sweep over his face.

"You're alright?" Kadian asked Jules, studying her face.

"I'm better. Dr. Van Pelt let me go." Jules replied, walking over to the wheel to stand near the Captain.

"You gave us all quite a scare. I'm glad to see that you're okay." He let out a sigh and turned his gaze back to the heavens before him.

"Where are we going? Henry said Nicodemus found a planet and moon where we can hide." She looked over at him questioningly.

"He did indeed. Good man. We're nearly there." He reached over to a small panel on a stand near him and pressed an intercom button, then flipped switches for 'Engine Room', 'Observatory', 'Flight Deck', and 'Lab'. Only those rooms would hear him speak. "Repair team, we're on approach. Report to Bridge."

Jules, Henry, and Finn could see the planet and the moon coming up just before them. They were both small. The planet was smaller than Earth's moon, and the moon was a fraction of the size of the planet.

"That planet looks like it's all desert!" Henry mused aloud. The door of the Bridge opened just then, and Nicodemus walked into the room. "It is a desert planet, and a saltwater moon."

"A what?" Henry asked, peering at the orange desert sands that covered the planet, and hoping for a glimpse of the moon which was on the other side of it.

"The moon is all saltwater, like a sea." Nicodemus explained. Henry was astounded.

"What a great juxtaposition." He murmured.

One by one, and then in groups of two or three, the repair team came onto the Bridge, assembling throughout the room.

When it seemed like most of the crew was there, the Captain spoke in a clear, loud voice. "Roll call!" He began, putting the ship into a hover position between the planet and the moon.

"Aeronautical Engineer!" Kadian called out.

"Present!" answered Oliver Corliss, whose sandy blonde hair looked as though it hadn't been combed in a week.

"Machinist."

"Present!" Shakti Sanna replied.

"Electrotech Officer."

"Here!" Tamsin Cuevas called out.

"Culturalist!"

"Present!" Trinity Barzetti piped up.

"Scientist!"

"Paisley Parker, here!" She raised her hand slightly.

"Astronomer."

"Nicodemus Hawking, here!" He answered, giving a smile to the children. The Captain knew he was there, but he would go through the whole list to make it official, as the meeting was being officially documented on the ship's computer.

"Meteorologist!"

"Samuel Calhoun, present!" Samuel answered smoothly.

"Inventor."

"I'm here." Marina responded with a smile, looking down at Sprocket who was still in dog form and had come to her feet.

"Flight Chief!"

"Lukas Tendaji, present." Tendaji stated firmly.

Captain Aragon gave a nod. "Good. Everyone is present and accounted for, for the record. Now, we need to get this ship back in order as quickly as possible. Nicodemus, what do we know about this planet and this moon?"

Nicodemus raised his voice somewhat. "Gypsy, please show a 3D display of the planet and moon." He told the ship's computer. A full color 3D display formed in the middle of the room, at eye level with the astronomer, about the size of the arm-span of two men. The crew gathered around it.

"The planet is all desert, made of orange Beluvian sand. It's toxic to humans. This moon, which is in orbit around the planet, is all saltwater. Because of the strength of the gravity on the planet, we'd need to be at least as far away as the moon to be at a safe distance to work without danger of toxicity from the sands."

Samuel spoke then. "The planet has high temperatures in the light of its sun, and very cold temperatures on its dark side. There are sand storms that will come up, with winds so high that entire planet will be covered in the blasting sand, it is a hostile environment. The saltwater moon has five hours of darkness and five hours of light. If we were to try to put the ship on the water, and it worked, we would have to sail at a constant speed in a forward motion to stay in the light so that we didn't have darkness, and we could get all of the repairs done."

Paisley pulled a device out of the purple shoulder bag she was wearing and touched the moon with her finger, enlarging it. Then she held the device up close to 3D digital image and studied the readings on it. "The salinity of the water is higher than the oceans of Earth, but not higher than the Dead Sea, so we'd be safe there. We could land the ship on it and sail in the daylight, as Samuel said. There is enough oxygen and gravity on the moon that we could drop the gravity and oxygen shield to repair it as well, because early reports show that it was partly compromised."

Shakti spoke up then. "It was compromised, and there is damage all along both the port and starboard sides of the ship. The Shimmer shield is inoperable, so we would have no cover of invisibility, the gravity and oxygen shield are operable but damaged, and four sections of the balloon have tears in them. My crew and I can have these things fixed, but we'll need some time. Maybe two days or less, if we have extra help."

"Many of the gauges and instruments were damaged in the Hollow, not by the attack, but by the magnetic storm in the Hollow, because the ship was weakened. I'll need a day to work on those with the tech ratings crew to get those up and running again." Tamsin reported.

"Then let's land on that saltwater moon and get these repairs done. You have the help of the full crew for any of your needs, just let James Dahl know, and our Steward will direct people where they need to be. Trinity!" Captain Aragon called out to her. She stepped out from the other side of the hologram of the moon suspended in the middle of the Bridge.

"Yes, Captain!" She answered.

"I want analysis work and mapping done of the moon, the planet, and as much of the region as we are able to read. This is unknown territory to us, and we need all the data that we can obtain on it. Take Nicodemus and Samuel with you on an exploration mission, and if Paisley has time, she should go as well. The Gypsy is our first priority, but while we're here, we must try to analyze and document all that we can about this place." Kadian ordered.

Trinity glanced at the children and spoke up. "Sir, would it be alright to take the children along with us on the exploratory mission? It would be no trouble to us, they could help us collect samples and analyze data, and it would keep them out of the way of the repairs."

Jules, Henry, and Finn all perked up as Trinity winked at them. Kadian looked over at the children. "That sounds like a fine idea. Children? Would you want to go?"

All three of them nodded eagerly. "Yes please!" They chorused.

"That's set, then. Trinity, they are with you on your team. The rest of you, let's land this ship and get to work. August, take her to the moon." Kadian looked over at his first mate, and August nodded and steered the Gypsy Windlass toward the saltwater, shining before them.

Before anyone had taken five steps, the door of the Bridge was flung open, and Anneliese Prichard stood panting in the doorway, her normally prim and tidy bun of dark hair at the back of her head was terribly askew, and her wide dark eyes were somehow even bigger.

"Sir!" She looked straight at the Captain. "I picked up a signal! There was a coded transmission sent to the Wraith galaxy! It had to have been sent from the other ship that we battled, but I can't figure out how the message got out of the Hollow. It isn't possible that a message could have originated from there because of the magnetic interference, but somehow it was definitely sent. I had to work at it, but I was able to break the code. It was a message to the Commodore that the Gypsy was coming to Wraith! I confirmed that the signal was received at its target." She stopped and drew in a deep breath, speaking more seriously and slowly then. "They know that we are coming, Sir."

The Captain turned and looked at the whole crew around him. "You heard her. Double time! Go now! First order of business, get that Shimmer device up and running! We must be able to be cloaked, because we're going to need it! Go!"

There wasn't a moment's hesitation. The entire crew dispersed and Trinity took the children with her, heading to their cabin.

"Dress for cool weather; wear layers, and bring a change of clothes in case you get wet. You'll need water resistant material and windbreakers. Take a scarf. Pack all that in the shoulder bags that I gave you, and let's go." She helped Finn pack her bag as Henry and Jules readied themselves. In minutes they were heading down the hall and into the depths of the ship.

As they entered the storage hull, the children looked around in wonder. It was a huge space, like a small warehouse, that was only partly filled with supplies and staples at one end of it. The rest of it was empty except for the far end, where one of the bay doors was. In that space was an exploratory pod. It was circular in shape, resembling the balloon on the deck, with small round doors on either side of it. It could easily fit ten people, and had a few simple amenities such as a miniscule kitchenette outfitted with tinned and hydrated food. The kitchenette also served as a half laboratory. There was a fresh water supply, a toilet room, and ten thick, wide chairs that could fold back into cots. There were windows all around the top and most of the sides, making it look more like an elongated bubble than a ship.

"We haven't been down here in the hull before, and we haven't seen this craft yet. This is incredible!" Henry exclaimed, his eyes moving swiftly over everything around them.

Trinity smiled at the children and held out her hand toward the pod. "May I present, the Pearl. She's our exploratory pod. She is equipped to be fully operational apart from the Gypsy for up to two earth weeks of time.

She opened the door and the children got in and looked around. There was an instrument panel every bit as sophisticated and technologically advanced as the Bridge on the ship, though much smaller.

"She's a mini version of the gypsy in many aspects. Marina, Shakti, Corliss, Tamsin, Paisley, Nicodemus, and Samuel all made her that way." Trinity beamed happily as she got onboard and began to prepare the Pearl for takeoff.

Minutes later, the rest of their small crew; Nicodemus, Samuel, Paisley, and Sprocket as a dog arrived and came on board.

"Are we ready?" Trinity asked, looking over her shoulder at the crew. Everyone was buckled in, and answered that they were ready.

"Let's go!" She called out excitedly. She pressed a button on the instrument panel before her, and the bay door opened. When it was fully accessible, a green light appeared over the door, and Trinity pushed the accelerator lever forward slowly. The engine purred, and the Pearl lifted easily off the floor of the hull, and zoomed out into space.

The ship was close to the moon, and they were able to watch from a short distance at the Gypsy Windlass splashed down into the sea, sailing toward the light as Tendaji adjusted the sails and somewhere in the Engine Room, Corliss set the engine speed.

"Mapping, investigative analysis, and diagnostics recording." Samuel reported.

Trinity pushed the accelerator lever forward again and the pod zipped toward the surface of the saltwater moon. The children grew wide eyed and breathless as the surface of the water came ever closer, until they splashed down into it, and the pod was entirely submerged.

"Does this pod leak?" Henry asked, reaching his hand out to the glass window beside him.

"Not a drop." Trinity answered. She's tight as a drum."

"Visibility at fifteen feet." Paisley stated, checking the gauges on the panel before her.

"Adjusting speed to coincide." Trinity replied, slowing the pod down.

There was nothing around them but seawater, as far as they had seen to that point. "I'm not getting any readings of life forms yet, but it is feasible that life could exist in these conditions." Paisley checked the computer and made some adjustments on it to be sure.

"There's a cave!" Finn called out from three rows back. She was as close to the side window as she could be without getting out of her seat.

Everyone looked, and saw that Finn was right. Just off to the starboard side of the craft was a huge cave.

"Well spotted, Finn! Nice work. Let's go have a look!" Trinity turned the pod toward the mouth of the cave and they sailed in easily. "Gosh, you could get the Gypsy in here without coming close to the edges. This is as big as our cave back on the island!"

They followed along through a tunnel that wound further in and downward, but never got smaller.

"The temperature has risen two degrees." Paisley stated. "We're coming closer to the core."

"There's something glowing up ahead!" Jules cried out. All eyes shifted to the front window.

"So there is!" Nicodemus smiled, peering at it.

They came upon it quickly, and found themselves in a big cavern. All around them on every side were glowing seashells the size of a large man's hand. They were formed into different shapes, but they were all of the same iridescent, glimmering material.

"Those are so beautiful." Trinity said, gazing at them as they floated in the center of the cavern. The seashells were attached to the rock walls of the cave in every place.

"What is that?" Henry asked, listening intently.

"What do you hear?" Paisley asked, trying to listen, herself.

"I'm not sure…" Henry paused and listened closer. "It sounds like some kind of… music or song."

Trinity spoke in a soft voice. "Turning up exterior microphones and interior speakers."

As she did so, everyone in the pod was able to hear a softly playing song. Paisley leaned forward and stared hard at the shells. "Trinity, pull the pod closer to them, please." Trinity approached the nearest wall of seashells.

"I believe they're vibrating!" Paisley said quietly with a smile. "That's where the song is coming from. They're vibrating, and the movement creates the song."

They listened for a little while, recording audio and visual as the analysis systems ran. Trinity held her hand up and looked at the others. "They're communicating. That vibration is a form of communication. What do you think, Paisley?" She asked, shifting her eyes to the scientist.

"I believe you're right. That has to be a form of communication for them. Let's get sample analysis." Paisley stood up and began to walk to the back of the pod. "You three should come with me, and you can help." She smiled at them.

The children followed her to the kitchen and lab area, and she showed them which buttons to push to open the exploratory arm, reach it out, and use it to bring some of the shells into the pod.

They examined their samples, studied them and made documentation about their findings, and then returned them to the same spots where they'd found them. The children couldn't be more enthralled, and even Rastaban helped out by pressing buttons and analyzing, loving every moment of the adventure.

The team followed the tunnel as it led away from the cavern at the center, and discovered that the tunnel emptied out on the other side of the moon.

"It's just one big hole right through the middle of the moon!" Finn exclaimed in surprise as they realized where they'd been.

"It is indeed." Nicodemus told her. "This is a fascinating discovery. I've got the charts all finished. They're being uploaded to the Gypsy now."

"Then let's go to the planet for a quick analysis. I don't see any other life forms in the water or anywhere in the air around the moon." Trinity announced, and they all agreed.

"Oxygen masks and biosuits on, everyone." Paisley instructed. "We have to be conscientious about being extra safe, this planet is a dangerous place. We're only going there long enough to get some samples, analyze the terrain and atmosphere, and make a map. Then we get back to the ship."

All of them wore oxygen masks and biosuits, and the children were amazed that the biosuits could expand or contract to fit the person who was wearing them. Paisley explained that Marina made them that way so that no matter who was in the pod, the suits would fit anyone who needed to wear them.

They left the saltwater moon and headed for the bright, burning orange sands of the sunny side of the planet. The contrast of the sand against the deep blue sky was breathtaking, and all of them commented on it.

Samuel created maps as they flew over the planet, and Nicodemus ran the analysis systems and recordings. The children and Rastaban helped Paisley collect sealed samples of the highly toxic Beluvian sand, and Trinity piloted the pod. They had gone halfway around the planet when Samuel raised his voice so everyone could hear him.

"The winds are picking up. There's a sandstorm building not far away. We need to leave now so that we don't get caught in it. If we do get caught in it, there's no way we'll ever get off of this planet alive." He spoke seriously.

"Finishing sample collections now." Paisley replied, and the children helped her put the samples away and bring the mechanical arm back into the ship and close the doors.

"Everyone buckle up and let's go!" Trinity called out. All of them put their safety harnesses on over their biosuits, and she lifted the craft away from the planet in strong winds just as the sandstorm was about to reach them.

Samuel whistled and gave his head a shake as a swirl of orange sand nearly got them. "Not a second too soon."

She smiled at him. "You gave us just enough time, Samuel. We make a good team; all of us. Great job everyone!"

They returned to the ship and docked the Pearl, all of them talking about what they had seen and discovered as they headed back to the lab. The children helped to upload the information they had into the computers, and then they were released for free time, as long as they didn't get in the way of the repairs.

Finn smiled shyly at Henry and Jules. "What if we get some popcorn from the kitchen and go to the cabin to watch another movie?" She suggested hopefully. "I really like movies."

They got popcorn and headed for their room, curling up in their robes and pajamas on the sofa and chair to watch a movie.

As Jules was opening and pouring their drinks for them, Henry looked at Finn and smiled. "You did really well today in the pod. It made me wonder what you might like to do when you grow up. What do you think?"

Finn gave it careful consideration. "Well, in my time, girls grew up to be wives and mothers, or they did laundry for other people, or cooked or cleaned, or they sewed. There wasn't much a girl could do. Now I know I could do anything, if I wanted to and I learned about it. So, I think I would want to be an inventor like Marina, or a scientist like Paisley. They're amazing."

"You could do it." Jules told her. "You could be anything you wanted, even the Captain of your own ship someday, I'm sure."

She handed the drinks out and looked at Henry. "What about you, brother? What would you like to do?"

Henry didn't hesitate at all. "I want to go work in the Universal Library with Rastaban." Upon hearing him, Rastaban, who was lounging in his garden box, looked up at Henry and smiled.

"I would love it if you did. I could certainly use an apprentice. You're welcome to the job at anytime, my lad. Anytime."

Jules smiled wide at him. "There would be no end of books or reading for you." She took her seat beside Finn on the sofa. "I think I want to do what my mother did. I want to be a Time Guardian. I need to know more about it first, but that's what I really want to do. I feel drawn to it."

Henry nodded. "You'd be amazing at it, sister." He looked at her proudly.

"The movie is starting!" Finn bounced a little with excitement.

The repairs were done in a day and a half, and the children spent some time lounging with movies, and some time helping with whatever repairs they could assist with. Finally, everything was working better than it had before, and it was time to get back into space and head to the Wraith galaxy.

They hadn't gone far when Henry, who was standing on the deck observing the space around them, called out and pointed to a distant spot in the darkness. "There was a flash! A flash!"

Nicodemus was standing near him. "Where? What kind of flash?" He asked, pushing his spectacles up on his nose and peering out at the darkness.

Another flash lit up close to the same area and then disappeared. "That looks like a Hollow closing!" Henry proclaimed, remembering what the flash looked like when they'd come out of the Hollow into the Atlas galaxy.

Nicodemus drew in a sharp breath. "You're right, they are both Hollows, and they were both used." He pushed a button on the copper bracelet at his wrist and spoke quickly.

"Captain, Henry and I have just seen two Hollows open and close, and there are ships coming through them." He said gravely.

An instant later, Captain Aragon was on the intercom to the whole ship. "Alert! Shimmer shield up immediately, power down everything except auxiliary functions, and everyone to your stations! We are in enemy territory."

Henry panicked, thinking of the girls who were back in the cabin, having fallen asleep during the last movie they watched. "I need to go to the cabin!" He told Nicodemus, who was headed to the Observatory.

The old man nodded. "Go! Stay alert and be ready for anything!"

Henry rushed back to the cabin and woke the girls. They dressed and pulled their shoulder bags out of the closet. Jules had come up with the idea that their shoulder bags should be packed with necessities in case anything happened. They were all glad that they were a little more prepared.

"Do you want to go up on deck? I can't stand being down here, not knowing what's going on." Jules pleaded, looking at the other two.

"Agreed, as long as we stay together." Henry told her, taking Finn's hand in his. They headed up to the deck and found the lights dimmed to almost nothing, and a silence that made them shiver.

Kadian, Nicodemus, Samuel, Marina, and Trinity were standing together. August was on the other side of the deck, opposite them. Sprocket had taken the form of the dragon again and went to the children, staying with them where they were behind Kadian. Wilson Ryers, the Chief Warrant Officer and Master at Arms was nearby, along with Harley Silverstein. Everyone else was at another station on the ship.

Three more Hollows opened, flashing across the black expanse of the Universe, and the crew could see an armada of ships emerge from them. There was silence on the Gypsy Windlass.

Samuel spoke quietly. "We are in what is a magnetic storm central, which is where all the Hollows are coming from. It's a clever place to put a hideout for time pirates; it makes the travel back and forth from far reaches of the Universe much easier."

The armada appeared to head toward the center of the Wraith galaxy in the distance. The crew still couldn't see it, but they knew where it was. It was the only place in the sky where there was nothing but darkness, ringed by light, filled with dark matter, and hidden from view.

Just as the crew and Captain were about to breathe a sigh of relief, the three biggest ships came straight for them.

A quiet message came through on the Captain's copper bracelet. "Artillery and gunners here, Sir!" They spoke low. "Do we have permission to fire?"

Captain Aragon looked around the ship and gazed long at his crew and the children behind him. "Hold your fire." He commanded grimly.

The three large metallic airships sailed up to the Gypsy and the biggest of them stopped right alongside it. The entire ship was black, save for large silver letters that spelled out its name over the bow, just beneath the Grim Reaper whose form was carved in iron at the head of the vessel.

Kadian groaned. "Oh no… that's Cerberus."

"What's Cerberus?" Henry asked in a whisper.

"In Greek mythology, Cerberus was the three headed dog that guarded the gates to the underworld… to hell. Right now it's the Commodore's ship. Commodore Winter Valen."

It seemed as if no one on the Gypsy was even breathing, they were all being so quiet. Sprocket changed into a dragonfly and rested on Jules' shoulder.

Marina leaned over to the children and pointed to the hidden panel for the secret passageway that the children had used on their first day aboard. They understood and gave her a quick hug before hurrying with dragonfly Sprocket to the secret panel and pressing the button. It opened noiselessly and they slipped inside, watching with the panel door open only a few inches.

A metallic plank formed, stemming from the adjacent ship and connecting with the Gypsy. The crew watched in silence as the plank suddenly flooded with wicked looking pirates, and each member stayed their ground as the pirates swarmed the ship, going to every person they could see and holding them hostage with one weapon or another.

Jules quickly closed the panel and pointed to an air vent that they could see the deck from. All three of them moved to peek out of it.

A large, cruel, crazy looking man strode arrogantly across the plank, taking his time, planting his boots with metal soles loudly so that his steps sounded like thunder.

His hair was a wild tuft, ragged and unruly, sticking out in every direction. His thin eyebrows were arched at the center and raised high, and he had a wide toothy grin on his face, as if he was caught between being deliriously happy and insanely angry. There was unease in all the men around him, including his own.

He got to the end of the ramp and stepped onto the Gypsy Windlass, gazing at everyone slowly, as if looking at them deeply would give him ownership of them.

Captain Aragon groaned. "Commodore Valen." He spoke in a low tone as a dagger was held to the side of his throat by a time pirate.

The Commodore let out an evil laugh; short and cold, and then proceeded to parade around the deck once, in an observatory march, glaring with disgust at each of the crew members, until he came to the Captain.

Winter Valen stopped fully in front of Kadian, and clasped his hands behind his back. He spoke with a slow sing-song sort of rhythm. "Well, Kadian… look at you, alive and well before me. We all thought that you were killed in the battle, but here you are, standing here as bold as brass on the grandest ship I've ever seen." He laughed with icy irony and gave his head a wild shake.

"How did you find us?" Kadian asked him evenly, showing no fear at all.

Commodore Valen leaned closer to the Captain, speaking slowly in a deep and menacing tone that everyone could hear. "Oh, we've perfected the art of finding what's hidden, much like you, stealing into Wraith. Let me take you the rest of the way."

Turning to the crew of the Gypsy, he walked up to August Holt and stared into his eyes. "Good work, Mister Holt. Thank you for sending that coded message. We wouldn't have been able to find them without your help in giving us the coordinates of the ship. I have half a mind to keep this pretty boat for myself, but I'm partial to Cerberus. A deal is a deal. I suppose there is some honor among thieves." He laughed frostily again. "The Gypsy Windlass is yours, and everyone aboard her except you, is mine. I'll send your new crew over from one of the runner ships."

Kadian stared at August in disbelief, and shook his head. "It can't be! August... tell me this isn't really happening!"

"It's Captain Holt to you." August answered coldly as he turned and walked alone toward the Bridge.

The children stared in horror. "It was August who sent the message to the Commodore, not the other ship! That makes sense." Henry whispered, "I thought it was Ferdie and Ox, but they wouldn't have told the Commodore where we were because they wanted to take us to Asterisma. Remember Anneliese couldn't figure out how a message could have made it out of the Hollow to the Commodore? That's because it didn't come out of the Hollow from the other ship! Now I can see it all. August waited until the other ship was around so it wouldn't look suspicious, and as soon as we came out of the Hollow, he sent the coded message from this ship! He's been working for the other side the whole time! He told the Commodore that we were coming, the scoundrel!" Henry was furious, as were Jules and Finn.

One of the time pirates turned then and looked around at the air vent, as if he thought he might have heard something there. The children held their hands over their mouths, their eyes wide with horror as they watched the crew of the Gypsy Windlass, including Kadian Aragon, be taken forcefully onto Cerberus, leaving the ship empty.

Stepping as silently as they could, they made their way down the secret passage until they came to a place far below the deck.

"Did August see us come into the passageway?" Henry asked, trying to remember.

"I don't think so." Jules answered, "He was on the other side of the deck when we ducked in here."

"What are we going to do?" Finn asked fearfully, looking from Henry to Jules and back again.

Jules let out a heavy sigh. "We're going to lay low. They can't leave this ship out in space. August will have to take it into Morden, even if it's only to restock, and Shady said that all the ships were being docked there because something big was coming. If August is a part of it, he'll have to be there, too. So, for now we're going to stay hidden on this ship until we can get to Morden and rescue our friends and Aunt Vianne."

Henry nodded. "We can do it, as long as we're together."

"Always." Jules replied, and they embraced each other.

Chapter Ten

~

Version Two

The pounding of feet startled Jules, and she drew in a deep breath, struggling to open her eyes. There were faces swimming over her head, all of them speaking to her swiftly and urgently. She felt hands on her arms and neck, holding her head and touching her forehead.

"What..." she tried to say, blinking as everything began to come back into focus. "What happened?"

She saw Corliss, Tamsin, Mel, and Henry all hovering over her. Pushing her hands against the hard floor, she slowly brought herself up to a sitting position.

Corliss frowned and searched her eyes, checking her pupils. "You fell when the ship got blasted, and you hit your head on the engine base."

"Ow..." She reached her hand up and rubbed the growing bump on the back of her head, but as she did so, she remembered what was happening, and her eyes opened wide in fear. "Oh no! Are we still under attack?"

Corliss stood up and looked around. "I'm not sure. Nothing is... moving right now..." He trailed off quietly and checked the monitors. "Except us. We're moving right now. That's strange. We shouldn't be out of the Hollow yet. At least, I think we shouldn't. Maybe the blast pushed us out faster. I need to run a diagnostic quickly to see if we're..." he trailed off without finishing his sentence as he worked.

Henry reached for Jules. "I was terrified when you went flying! I saw you hit your head and it was awful! We all heard it. I thought you were killed." He wiped at a tear in his eye and a small smile of relief turned up the corners of his mouth.

"Is she okay? Can I get out of this seat now?" Finn called from across the room.

Jules leaned around Henry's shoulder and lifted her hand, giving Finn a little wave. "I'm okay! I'm okay." She groaned and rubbed her head again. "I think." She looked over at Henry.

Mel and Tamsin helped her to her feet. Tamsin gave her shoulder a light rub. "You're a lucky girl. You could have really been hurt. It's so important to be buckled up. One of us should have taken care of Finn, and you should have stayed buckled into your seat. No real harm done though, so we'll get back to work, and you can take a seat until you're not dizzy anymore."

Jules shook her head. "I'm not diz-" she paused and raised one brow. "Yeah, I guess I better take a seat."

"This can't be possible." Corliss said, running his hands over the control console and then standing back up and crossing his arms over his chest. He lifted his hand to his mouth and chewed on the end of this thumb.

"Gypsy!" He said aloud to the ship's computer. "Double check the location."

"Confirmed." Answered the ship's computer.

He furrowed his brow. "Not possible. That's not..." He trailed off again and planted his hands on his hips.

"What is it?" Henry asked interestedly.

"We're not where we intended to be. Not even close." Corliss pressed an intercom button. "Bridge! Bridge, this is Corliss."

"Corliss, where are we, and why don't I have any control over the ship? Did we get out of the Hollow okay?" Kadian's voice came over the intercom in frustration.

Jules' heart began to race and she leaned over and shot her brother a worried look. "Oh no! Remember they said that people can get trapped in a Hollow and there's no way out, ever? What if we're trapped?" Panic laced her voice and Henry's eyes grew wide.

"I don't know why we don't have control of the ship, but I do know that we're not in the Hollow any longer." Corliss answered with a groan.

"Well where are we?" Kadian demanded irritably.

"We're in the Milky Way."

There was a silence at the other end of the intercom for a long moment. "We're *where*?" Kadian gasped. "How could we possibly be in the Milky Way? That's... that's home, right back where we started!"

"Actually, very close to where we started. The ship is headed for Earth, as near as I can tell." Corliss admitted miserably.

Jules got out of her seat and walked to the window. The ship was sailing steady and straight forward. Henry got out of his seat and helped release Finn, and they joined her at the window.

"Are you sure the ship's positioning system wasn't bungled by the Hollow?" Kadian pressed.

"Sir, our location is confirmed. We are coming up rapidly on our own solar system." Corliss sighed and turned around to look at Tamsin. "Is everything running as it should be?"

"Yes." She nodded in dismay. "I don't know how we got here, but everything is just as it should be."

"Except that we're not in control of the ship. Right?"

Tamsin gave Corliss another nod. "Right."

He frowned. "Well, if we're not in control of it, then someone else is. Check to see if we're caught in a tractor beam or something like that."

Tamsin turned back to her machines and her fingers flew over the dials, buttons, and switches. The computer beeped and she hung her head down low as she leaned over the panel beneath her. "We're in a tractor beam. I hadn't thought of that, or I'd have checked for it, but that's what's wrong. That's why we have no control."

Jules gasped as she looked out of the window. "Look! Henry look! It's the Sentinel Stars!"

Henry narrowed his eyes. "What are the Sentinel Stars?"

Rastaban, sitting with his fluffy head outside of Henry's pocket, perked up. "They're the four stars that guard the Time Palace. We are nearly home."

"Well who has a tractor beam on us? Who's pulling us in?" Corliss asked, trying to make some sense of it all.

Jules turned to look at him with a serious expression. "Corliss, look. It's the Sentinel Stars. They guard the Time Palace. We're sailing in past the Sentinel Stars, and because we're getting past them, that means we must be being brought into the Time Palace."

He covered his face with his hands and sighed heavily. When he lowered his hands again, he spoke up. "Did you hear that, Captain? Did you hear Jules?"

"I did." Came the reply over the intercom.

Then the Captain turned on the ship's intercom, so that everyone could hear him. "Attention. All hands on deck, immediately. We are on approach to the Time Palace."

Minutes later, everyone was on deck as requested, and the ship sailed smoothly into one of the ship bays at the Time Palace. It was far more elegant than the Port of Morrow.

"Well, it looks as though they're expecting us." Kadian grumbled as he looked out onto the dock. Jules, Henry, and Finn stood at his side.

There on the dock was the Empress herself, with a huge host of people behind her, and a few guards in front of her.

"What's all that about?" August asked, staring at the crowd. "Did you break a law I don't know about yet?"

Kadian shot him a dark look.

August shrugged as if he didn't know what could possibly be wrong with what he had said.

"Lower the ramp. They brought us in. Let's see what they want." Kadian ordered. The ramp was lowered, and the main crew and the children disembarked the ship, walking onto the dock and standing together before the Empress.

"Kadian Aragon." The Empress began, speaking with the same cool tone she had spoken to Jules with, and looking as calm as she had the last time the children had seen her.

"Yes, Empress." Kadian answered her.

She turned and looked at Jules and Henry. "And the Starling children."

Jules took a few steps toward her. "How did we end up here? Was it because the instruments malfunctioned in the Hollow?"

"No." The Empress replied evenly. "You're here because I brought you here. We've uncovered the whereabouts and the identity of the Commodore of the time pirates. We have a rescue mission currently in progress."

Jules and Henry brightened. "You're going to save Aunt Vianne?" Henry asked with high hopes.

"Yes." The Empress said. "She should be here soon." Then she held her hand out to Jules. "In the meantime, I will be confiscating your Cerellus as it does not belong to you yet. You will return it to me immediately. You did not store it in the box that I gave to you and instructed you to keep it in, so you will no longer be allowed to keep it in your possession."

Jules felt her heart nearly pounding out of her chest, and she reached her hand to the pendant sphere hanging around her neck, hidden just under her vest. She closed her fingers around it tightly.

"Your little friend there, whom you brought back with you from the past, will be returning to her home there. She never should have been taken out of her time. That is strictly against the rules. If you had gone through any of the training required of a proper, registered Time Guardian, you would have known that. The consequences of taking anyone out of their own time are severe, because the ripple effects through time can be disastrous. How do you know that she wasn't intended to have a considerable impact in her own natural lifetime? You don't, and you took her from it and decided to keep her in this time. It's absolutely not allowed. She will be taken back right away." The Empress' cool voice took an icy turn.

Finn grabbed tight to Henry and Jules' hands. "No! I don't want to go back! I ain't going back! There's nothing for me there!"

The Empress shook her head. "There's nothing for you here. This isn't your time or place." Then she turned to Kadian. "And *you*." She stated callously. "You are under arrest for interference and kidnapping. You had no right whatsoever to take those children, nor to interfere with the search for Vianne Starling."

Kadian's mouth fell full open. "What? Arrest? But, you can't... you don't understand! Vianne and I-" he began, but the Empress held up her hand and cut him off.

"It does not matter what you were. The simple fact is that it was not up to you to go and try to rescue her. She is a Time Guardian, she is one of the best guardians we have, and she is under the full protection of the Time Palace. You never should have gone after her, and you absolutely never should have taken the children. Their existence was a well kept secret until you dragged them off into space with you on your quest, kidnapping them from their home. I was sending guardians to care for them until we had Vianne back safe again. Now half the Universe is aware that those two children exist, and *you* have put their lives in mortal danger!" The Empress was visibly furious with Kadian over his carelessness with the children.

He clenched his jaw and took a step toward her. "We were nearly there! We found out where the Commodore was, and we were on our way to rescue her! If we'd gotten there first, you wouldn't have anything to say about it!"

"Oh, I'd still have plenty to say about it. Guardians, arrest him and his crew, and collect the girl. She's going back to her time immediately." The Empress gazed at Kadian unblinking, as the horde of Time Guardians behind her rushed them, binding them and closing their hands in irons.

Everything seemed to be happening in slow motion from Jules' perspective. She watched in horror as Kadian was knocked to the ground and shackles were clamped on his ankles and wrists. Nicodemus and Trinity were bound and arrested, followed by Jonathon, James, Samuel, and Corliss. The rest of the crew was being taken down and Kadian looked straight at her.

"Run!" He yelled to her. "Run, if you can!" She knew what he meant. He meant Finn. She and Henry would be fine; nothing would happen to them, but Finn would be taken back to her time, and left there alone. They had to run. Jules looked around and panicked. There was nowhere to run to; they were at the Time Palace in space, and the closest place to them was Earth, and they had no way to get there.

Then she felt the sphere around her neck, still in her fingers, and she looked down at it as chaos reigned around her.

Her eyes shot up and she yelled to Finn and Henry, "Hold on to me now!" They both reached for her, their fingers closing tightly around her arms, and she pulled the Cerellus from beneath her vest. Pressing her fingertips to the globe inside, she gave it a sharp spin in reverse. Henry looked up at her in sheer panic.

"What are you doing? Do you know what you're doing?"

Jules shook her head. "No, I don't know, but I have to do something!" She spun it again, faster, and everything around them began to go backwards. It was as if they were in a bubble, and the whole Universe was outside the bubble, all of it going in reverse.

The guardians released the crew, their shackles fell off, and they all stood back up. Kadian was released. The guardians went back to their places behind the Empress, and all of it continued, but the whole while, the Empress did not change. She simply stood there and stared at Jules, her eyes locked on the girl.

They found themselves back on the ship, then headed backward in the tractor beam, and after a while, they were back in the Hollow. Jules continued to turn the sphere backward, and they retracted back through their battle with the other ship, and then they were on the deck watching Shady dangle over the side. He left the ship and they went backward through the Port of Morrow, unseeing and undoing everything that they had done.

Henry stared and then looked at her as it all moved around them. "Will we remember what happened the first time?" He asked curiously.

She shrugged. "I don't know."

Finally they were back on board the ship, just coming to a stop at the dock in the Port of Morrow, and she felt safe. She felt that she had gone back far enough.

Jules closed her fingers around the spinning globe, and stopped it where it was. Everything was still for a moment. Then she realized that everything was staying still for much longer than a moment, and her heart began to pound again. She looked over at her brother and Finn.

"No one is moving! Nothing is moving! Why isn't it undone? Why isn't everything moving the way that it should be?" She asked them fearfully, but they weren't moving either. Both of them were as frozen as everything else around her.

The only thing that did move was the figure off to the side of her. She turned, and saw the Time Empress. She was standing on the deck of the Gypsy Windlass as they were docked at the Port of Morrow. She walked toward Jules, her violet eyes locked on the girl, and an instant later, she was directly in front of her. The tall willowy woman closed her hand around the Cerellus and pulled it from Jules' neck, breaking the chain.

"Nothing is moving because you cannot change this."

Chapter Ten

~

Version Three

Jules opened her eyes and blinked, looking around. She was laying in her bunk, and Henry was sitting on the sofa, reading a book to Finn.

"Henry?" She asked, sitting up and immediately wincing. Lifting her hand, she rubbed her fingers over the back of her head where a throbbing pain pulsed.

Henry set the book down and went right to her, with Finn on his heels. "You're awake! How do you feel? Are you alright?" He sat beside her and Finn sat with them.

With a sigh, Jules lowered her hand. "I think I'm okay. I just have a headache."

"Dr. Van Pelt said that you would. He had you in sick bay for a little while just to make sure you were okay, but he said you're fine. You've just got a little bump on the head. He said you could take this and your headache would go away." Henry reached his hand up to his shirt pocket and Rastaban handed him a little pill wrapped in paper.

"Thank you, Rastaban." Henry smiled at the bookworm, and gave the pill to Jules.

"Where are we? What happened? Did we get out of the Hollow?" Jules' eyes grew wide with panic as everything came back to her.

Her brother nodded. "We did. We actually defeated the other ship in the Hollow, and then a weird thing happened. As the gunners were firing, they sent a really strong blast to the other ship, and that pushed us out of the Hollow and knocked the other ship back into it, so the other ship was trapped."

Jules mouth fell open and she gasped. "Wait, didn't they say that if anyone is ever trapped in a Hollow that it's forever? They can't get out?"

"That's what Corliss told us after we got out of it. The other ship will be trapped in there forever. No way out. Everyone started calling it Finn's Hollow, since she was the one who discovered it in the first place, and it really saved us all. I don't know if we would have survived the battle if the other ship hadn't been trapped. The Gypsy sustained some damage; the attackers did get some shots in before it was over. The crew are working on the repairs right now, actually. They say that when they're done, we'll be able to head to Wraith."

"How close did we get?" Jules perked up a little, hoping for the best.

A big smile formed over Finn's face. "The Hollow that I found was a really good one, I guess. Deep. So deep that it got us to the Atlas galaxy, where they wanted to go. Nicodemus told us we're right on the edge of the Wraith galaxy now. We just can't go on until they make repairs."

"They found it?" Jules grinned with elation. "That's fantastic!"

Henry gave a nod. "We did find it. It's really small, but we found it and we're on the cusp of it. We're kind of hiding in a nebula right now, laying low while they make repairs. It looks so cool outside; it's all green and cloudy. There's an eerie sort of glow to it."

"I like nebulas. I think they're pretty." Finn stated happily.

"I think they're pretty, too." Jules agreed with Finn, giving her a wink. "So, you two just sat here and waited for me to wake up?"

Finn brightened and drew in an excited breath. "We didn't just sit here doing nothing; Henry is teaching me how to read!"

Jules blinked as her mind spun. "You… you don't know how to read?"

"Nor write, neither, but I'll learn that too." Finn admitted honestly. "Where I come from, girls ain't worth much, except for being wives and mothers or working the fields. Sometimes they can get jobs like teachers or nurses if they're lucky. When we was in Ireland, we was on a farm. I never went to school; I was always working the land for the laird. When I was in New York, I learned to live on the streets, had to be smart about it, but it wasn't smart like books and reading and writing, it was smart to get by and be safe. Now I'm getting by and I'm safe, so I can learn to read and write. I always wanted to. It's so exciting!" She bubbled happily about it. Henry gave her a warm smile.

"You're doing really well with it. You are smart, and you're catching on fast." He gave her a pat on the back.

Jules shook her head. "It's astounding to me that women were ever treated so poorly and unequally, just because they were girls. That's unthinkable. I'm glad we've come so far, but it's clear that we still have a long way to go."

"Well I'm glad to be in a time now where women aren't property. I hated the idea of being owned, like a dog or a horse. I'm my own person now, and I ain't letting go of it." She lifted her chin and Jules and Henry both felt enormously proud of her.

Sprocket came through the door just then as an eagle, tall and fierce looking. "The repairs are being finished up and we'll be flying to Morden shortly." He reported. "We're going to save Vianne!"

The children cheered and followed Sprocket up to the deck. They found Kadian and August just coming off of the lift in the central shaft of the balloon.

Relief washed over Kadian's face when he saw Jules walking with Henry and Finn.

"You're alright!" He smiled at her and gave her shoulder a pat.

"I am." She nodded, smiling back at him.

"You gave us quite a scare, hitting your head like that. It could have gone very badly. It looks like all is well now, though. I'm glad you're on your feet again, because we're about to leave for Morden. The damage on the ship has been repaired, and we're making ready to sail. I'd like it if you and Henry, and of course Finn, would come to the Bridge with me when we sail in. We're going after someone who is very important to us all, and I feel that we should be together when we arrive." His sky blue eyes shone with a fondness for the children, and it crossed Jules' mind to wonder if he might ever consider marrying Vianne, which would make him her uncle.

"I'd love to!" She felt a thrill rush through her. Looking over at Henry and Finn, she raised a brow. "How about you two?"

"I'm in!" Finn almost bounced in place.

"Me too." Henry agreed. "I can't wait to see her. I miss her so much."

Kadian nodded. "Then let's go get her."

August, Kadian, and the children went to the Bridge, and they set course for the center of the Wraith galaxy. Nicodemus and Samuel joined them, and the ship left the dark side of the small moon where they had remained veiled, and Kadian called out for the Shimmer shield to be activated. A light ripple moved over the ship, and it was cloaked from everything outside of it.

The space around them appeared to grow darker, though it wasn't. It was merely the absence of light from stars, and though the temperature aboard the ship remained constant, there was a cold feeling about the vacuum they entered. The sheer emptiness around them seemed entirely devoid of life, as if they were the only existence in the Universe.

Henry shivered, and rubbed his hands over his arms, furrowing his brow as he looked out into the black abyss.

"Are you cold?" August asked, watching him.

"Not so much cold as… numb. There's nothing here, just… nothing at all. No light, no sound, no heat or fire, no life… it's chilling." He looked up at August in trepidation. "I hope we can get out of here fast."

Jules reached for his hand and held it in hers. "I know what you mean. Shady said this was a galaxy graveyard, but graveyards hold the remains of what once lived. There aren't even remains here. There's just… emptiness here. I don't even know how we'll find their Morden stronghold when we can't see anything at all out there."

Nicodemus turned toward her. "We'll find it by mass and gravity. There isn't mass around us right now, but we're taking readings and wherever they are hiding, there will be mass, and with mass comes gravity. The more mass something has, the more gravity it has. We'll find it, I have no doubt."

Jules felt a bit better about what Nicodemus told her, but the foreboding and unease that Henry felt continued to hang about them; a heavy and shadowed shroud.

It wasn't much later that Corliss called them from the Engine Room. "Captain, we're picking up a slight disruption in the radar. I think it might be what we're looking for. Are you getting that same reading?"

Kadian, August, Nicodemus, and Samuel all examined the monitors and readings. "That's it. It's small, but it's the only thing out there, and I'm willing to bet this ship that that's it. So well hidden. We're shifting course. Thank you, Corliss."

Captain Aragon stood at the ship's wheel and turned it just enough to put it on a direct path to the dense mass showing up on the monitors. "It looks like it might be a little while before we get there, but we're on our way."

The door opened then, and Katsuro came onto the Bridge. Captain Aragon and August turned to him. Katsuro gave the Captain a nod.

"I'd like to take children to studio for extra training. We don't know what we're headed into, and they will need all skills they can learn. One simple lesson may be enough to turn the tide and save their lives." He shifted his gaze from Kadian to Jules, Henry, and Finn.

Kadian looked at the monitors. "We have time. Take them. Teach them the best you can with the time you have. I'll notify you when we've gotten to the perimeter."

As Katsuro walked to the studio with the children, he talked with them.

"I was listening when we had Shady on ship. I believe he is right. We will have hard time making it in alive. If we get in, we will have difficult time making it back out again. I want to be certain you are prepared for anything that might happen. You are most valuable asset onboard ship." He gave them a half smile and they entered the studio.

Long lessons later, Kadian called the studio from the Bridge. "We're getting close. Send the children back up please."

Katsuro walked back with the children, who were plenty worn out from their workout. "You have done well. I feel more confident that if anything happens, you will be ready for it." He told them with a tone of pride.

They entered the Bridge and Katsuro stayed with them. Sprocket was still in the form of an eagle, big and bold, keeping an eye on everything around the ship.

Corliss called the Bridge from the Engine Room. "We're entering the edge of the mass now. I detect nothing near us, though from the readings, we should… coming up… it very…" The last part of what the engineer said was broken, and lost.

"Corliss!" Kadian called his name, speaking into the intercom.

There was no reply.

The lights on the Bridge and around the ship began to flicker.

"Corliss!" Kadian raised his voice. There was nothing but silence. The lights all over the ship went off and darkness surrounded them.

Kadian flipped on the intercom for the whole ship. "We're losing communications and lights. There is a disruption in power! Going to auxiliary immediately!" He flipped the switch for the auxiliary lights all over the ship. They were not electric lights, but rather an organic invention that Marina had created with a bioluminescent cellular structure. A soft turquoise glow showed around the edges of the ship in small areas few and far between, just barely breaking up the darkness.

"What's happening?" Henry asked worriedly, watching the men on deck scramble and the lights all over the Bridge go out, save for the auxiliary.

"I don't know." Kadian answered. "I'm not sure what's wrong with it."

Just then there was a voice on the Captains copper bracelet, the same bracelet that all crew on the ship wore for a communications link.

"Captain! Can you hear me? It's Corliss!"

"I'm here! What's going on? Status update!" Kadian commanded.

"The engines are down. Nothing is working in any part of the engine room. I can't get anything started again! We're dead in the water if we don't get it fixed! We'll be drifting, powerless!"

A strained look crossed Kadian's face. "We aren't dead in the water, and I don't think we're drifting, but we are moving."

"What do you mean, we're moving? We can't be moving. Nothing is on and running!" Corliss sounded completely confused.

"The ship is on course for the center of the mass, just as we were taking her, but even though the engines are off, even though everything is off, we are still moving toward our destination. In fact, if I was judging by the look of it without the monitors, I'd say that we were going faster than we were with the engines on, though I have no idea how." Kadian raked his hands through his hair in frustration, trying to figure it out.

Nicodemus walked toward the glass at the front of the Bridge, reaching out to touch it with his hand. "It has to be the gravity from the mass. The closer we get to the mass, the stronger the gravitational pull. If we don't get the engines and power back on again, we won't be able to leave." He turned and looked back at Kadian.

"Remember Samuel said that this is magnetic storm central? I think it's the magnetic storms throughout the area here that are interfering with the electronics on the ship. It's just like being in a Hollow, except it's not in one isolated spot, it's everywhere." There was more than a hint of fear in his eyes.

Kadian's eyes grew wide. "Do you mean to tell me that we're in one giant Hollow? Is it possible that we might be trapped in here?"

"It isn't like a Hollow," Nicodemus answered, "it's different, but similar. The time pirate's ships go in and out, so there has to be a way, but unless we figure out exactly what that way is, we're not going anywhere. We can't escape the gravitational pull without power, and we can't create power with electromagnetic interference, which is happening randomly all over the place throughout this area, with greater intensity than I've ever seen."

Henry cried out loudly then. "Ships! Look! There are ships right in front of us! There was nothing there a minute ago, absolutely nothing, and now… there are dozens of ships!"

Everyone stared out of the front window in alarm as an entire armada of black ships that were lit up with silvery light appeared out of nowhere, directly in front of the Gypsy Windlass.

Kadian spoke into his bracelet. "Anyone who can hear this, get to your stations immediately! Imminent attack! Imminent attack!"

No sooner had the words left him than the fleet around the Gypsy began to fire lasers at the ship, blasting it all around the front. There was only a thin shield to protect the ship, as it was on auxiliary power.

Kadian called on his bracelet to the gunners. "Fire! Fire back with everything we have! Shoot them with the knives from the kitchen if you have to, but hit them with something!"

He saw several of the crew on the deck, and yanked the Bridge door open. "I must go and fight with them! To the deck!"

The crew on the deck were firing shots from guns and hand lasers, and Katsuro vanished down into the studio and came back armed from head to toe with everything he could carry.

Jules, Henry, and Finn all ran to stand behind Kadian and the crew. When he saw them, he shouted over the sound of the battle.

"Get to a safe place!"

Jules shook her head. "There's no safer place than with you, and you wouldn't desert you're crew. You're fighting with them, and we are your crew, too! We're staying!"

He tried to argue with her, but it distracted him from the fight, and he was obligated to acquiesce. "Fine, but get down low and stay down!"

The children dropped low behind some crates on the deck and watched. "How can we help them?" Jules asked, frustrated that they weren't doing anything.

Henry thought for a moment and then brightened. "I know! The laser pointers that we have from the Observatory. We can shine those in the eyes of the enemy, and perhaps our crew can fire upon them more easily then! At the very least, we can be a considerable distraction!"

All three of them pulled their laser pointers out from their pockets and started aiming them at the faces that they could find on the decks of the other ships. It was a help by creating a target, and Paisley turned and shouted a loud thanks to them as she saw what they were doing.

Shoulder to shoulder with his crew, Kadian fired shots from his gun and ducked and dodged shots that were fired at him, for the time pirates who were attacking them were not only firing lasers from their ships, but were shooting their own guns from the decks as well.

The biggest ship of them all drew near the bow of the Gypsy Windlass, and Kadian's voice grew menacing. "The Commodore!" He shouted angrily, firing everything he had at the pirates on that deck.

The Commodore's ship blasted powerful lasers at the Gypsy, and with every hit, more and more of her was destroyed, from tears in the balloon to explosions all over the hull and bow, and then there was a great one that hit the deck.

The blast destroyed the area where many of the crew were, and as the children watched, several of them fell. Without a thought to their own safety, the children left their place behind the crates and rushed to their fallen mates.

"August! Nicodemus! No!!" Henry cried out in horror.

"Trinity and Paisley!" Jules echoed her brother as tears streamed down her face.

They were all killed, and many more were injured and on the brink of death. Among them was Kadian Aragon.

"Jules!" He called out, laying on his back and leaning to the side on one elbow. She saw him and ran to him with Henry and Finn just behind her. Dropping to her knees, she reached for his arm and shook her head.

"No! You can't be hurt! Get up!" She urged him desperately.

"Jules, listen to me now. You three get down to the Pearl in the hull and turn on the Shimmer for it. Escape out of the hatch. The technology on the Pearl is independent of the Gypsy, it shouldn't be too badly affected by the magnetic storms. Find a Hollow and take it. Get to the Time Palace. The Empress will help you. Take Sprocket with you." He cried out from the pain in his leg where he had been hit.

"We're not leaving you!" Jules insisted stubbornly, and Henry and Finn agreed.

Kadian shook his head and raised his voice. "No! You have to go, otherwise there is no chance for your survival! You said that you were part of my crew and that means you must obey my orders. I'm ordering you as your Captain, GO!"

There was nothing for it. The front of the ship was hit again, and everything around them shook terribly.

Part of the balloon fell and hit the front of the deck, falling over the bow of the ship.

Kadian gave them a pained and sorrowful look. "I'm so sorry. Now go, and may the luck of all the stars be with you."

Jules felt hot tears trailing down her cheeks and she was blinded by them as she turned and grabbed Henry's and Finn's hands, running with eagle Sprocket who flew overhead as they raced down the deck and then the stairs one floor after another, until they got down to the deep belly of the ship. They ran all the way to the back of the hull, where the little exploratory pod, the Pearl, sat.

Jules opened the door and they climbed in, along with Sprocket, and Rastaban, who was tucked safely into Henry's shirt pocket.

Jules searched for the way to start the pod, and grew frustrated as she was pressing buttons all over the control console. "Dang it, how do you get this thing started?" She cried out.

Everything came to life and lit up inside the pod. "Would you like me to start the engines?" Came a calm feminine voice. It was Marina's voice, coming from the computer.

Jules looked up and all around. "Yes?" She answered with uncertainty. The engine started.

"Can you open the hatch to get us out of here?" She asked. "Please?"

The ship's hatch began to open. Jules sighed in relief and looked at Henry and Finn who were each sitting in a chair. "Get your safety belts on now." She told them, snapping hers in place. They followed suit.

The Gypsy rocked and trembled again with another solid blow. "Turn on the Shimmer shield and get us out of here!" Jules called out, her eyes flooded with tears and her voice cracking as she spoke.

She felt Henry's hand on her shoulder. "I know. I don't want to leave them either, but we have no choice now, and you know it."

The pod zipped out of the ship and sailed silently into the darkness, going back the way that they had come.

"Can you find a Hollow?" Jules asked the computer.

"I can send the signals, and when you detect the irregularity that you're looking for, you can tell me which one it is, and I will set a coordinate for that location." The Pearl answered her.

"Do that, please." Jules replied. Then she turned and looked at Finn. "We're lucky to have a great Hollow finder with us. Work your magic, Finn. Listen for that irregularity and help us get to a Hollow."

They listened and waited. It wasn't long at all before Finn jumped in her seat. "I hear one! That's it… that one!"

"Did you get that, Pearl?" Jules asked, looking around at the control console. She wasn't sure where to look while she was talking to the ship.

"Affirmative. Location detected. I will direct the pod there immediately." The Pearl replied.

The Pearl turned then, and the children could see the Gypsy Windlass far out to one side of the ship. It was surrounded at the front and sides by the armada of time pirate ships. They could see lasers firing from every direction, and each shot tore into the ship, creating tremendous devastation all over it.

All three of the children and Rastaban wept as they watched helplessly. Flames and smoke poured from all over the ship, from places where it was broken and torn.

"Nearing the Hollow now." The Pearl announced calmly. "Entering in ten seconds."

They saw a huge blast fired from the Commodore's ship. It was the coup de grâce. The shot hit dead center of what was left of the Gypsy Windlass, and a split second later, the entire ship exploded, flames and debris flew in every direction, sailing off and leaving nothing behind.

"*NO!*" Every one of the children cried out, sobbing for the loss of all of their friends, their hands pressed tightly to the glass, wishing that they could reach out and grab every life silenced in the blast. Their hearts felt as if they had exploded just as the ship did, leaving only tatters in the wake of the devastation.

"Entering the Hollow in five seconds." The Pearl informed them in its serene voice.

Jules swallowed the lump in her throat and pressed her hand to her heart to try to stem the pain there. Her fingers touched on something solid.

She looked down and held up the Cerellus, her mouth falling open as realization dawned on her like a new day.

"Computer! Stop! Don't enter the Hollow! Stop! Stop! Stop!" she yelled loudly.

"Stopping." The computer replied. "Hollow evaded. Shall I search for another Hollow?"

Henry turned and looked at Jules in horror. "Have you lost your mind? What are you doing? The only thing left around here now are the time pirates and us, and we're lucky they haven't detected us! We're lucky this thing even works! If we don't get out of here right now, we'll die too! The Captain was trying to save our lives! Don't waste that gift by staying here! There's nothing that we can do for them now!"

"I'm going to turn time backward and save them all." Jules vowed determinedly.

Henry's mouth fell open and he stared at her. "You're going to do *what*?"

She turned and gave him a challenging look. "Are we Time Guardians or what?"

"We can't do that!" He shook his head in panic.

"We have to. We have got to go back and save our friends. We have no choice." Jules held the brass sphere up in her hands and taking a deep breath, spun the globe backward as fast as she could.

*Light years from
The End...*

Made in the USA
San Bernardino, CA
11 September 2017